#1 Teacher Recommended!

**BRIDGING GRADES
5 to 6**

Summer Bridge®
An imprint of Carson Dellosa Education
PO Box 35665
Greensboro, NC 27425 USA

© 2025 Carson Dellosa Education. Except as permitted under the United States Copyright Act, no part of this publication may be reproduced, stored, or distributed in any form or by any means (mechanically, electronically, recording, etc.) without the prior written consent of Carson Dellosa Education. Summer Bridge® is an imprint of Carson Dellosa Education.

Printed in the USA • All rights reserved.
ISBN 978-1-4838-7274-2
01-006251151

Caution: Exercise activities may require adult supervision. Before beginning any exercise activity, consult a physician. Written parental permission is suggested for those using this book in group situations. Children should always warm up prior to beginning any exercise activity and should stop immediately if they feel any discomfort during exercise.

Caution: Nature activities may require adult supervision. Before beginning any nature activity, ask parents' permission and inquire about the child's plant and animal allergies. Remind the child not to touch plants or animals during the activity without adult supervision.

Caution: Before completing any balloon activity, ask parents' permission and inquire about possible latex allergies. Also, remember that uninflated or popped balloons may present a choking hazard.

The authors and publisher are not responsible or liable for any injury that may result from performing the exercises or activities in this book.

Table of Contents

How to Use Your *Summer Bridge Activities* Book. 4
Skills Matrix 6
Summer Reading and Free E-books 8
Summer Reading Log 9
Section 1: Monthly Goals and Word List **10**
Introduction to Flexibility 11
Let's Play Today Activities 12
Activity Pages. 13
Science Experiments 53
Social Studies Activities 55
Section 2: Monthly Goals and Word List **58**
Introduction to Strength 59
Let's Play Today Activities 60
Activity Pages. 61
Science Experiments 101
Social Studies Activities 103
Section 3: Monthly Goals and Word List **106**
Introduction to Endurance 107
Let's Play Today Activities 108
Activity Pages. 109
Science Experiments 149
Social Studies Activities 151
Reflect and Reset 154
Answer Key 155
Flash Cards
Reference Chart

How to Use Your *Summer Bridge Activities*® Book

This *Summer Bridge Activities 5-6* book is designed to help your child have a smooth transition from fifth grade to sixth grade. The exercises in this book focus on fifth-grade practice and mastery and sixth-grade introduction. The skills covered in this book touch on all curriculum areas (reading, writing, math, science, and social studies) and take about 15 minutes per day. Let's get started!

Take it Month-by-Month

Your Summer Bridge Activities book is set up to mirror the three months of the summer. Have your child work their way through the book starting with Section 1 (the first month of their summer break), then on to Section 2 and Section 3 as the summer progresses.

Two Pages per Day in Just 15 Minutes!

Your child has two pages to complete each weekday (a front and a back), taking about 15 minutes total. The days and skills taught are clearly marked at the top for easy reference.

Healthy Habits for a Healthy You!

These short bonus bars will encourage your child to develop healthy physical and emotional habits and will foster a love of learning. They include:

Mindful Moments	Let's Play Today	Fast Fun Facts

Character development activities that focus on social and emotional learning	Activities that encourage physical activity and a sense of play	Fun trivia facts that encourage curiosity and a love of learning

The adventure continues online with IXL!

Throughout this edition of Summer Bridge Activities®, you'll see 3-digit codes that connect your family with fun, motivating online practice questions on IXL, the most widely used K-12 online learning program in the U.S. On IXL.com or the IXL mobile app, simply type the 3-digit code into the Skill ID box to start "playing" IXL and earning fun awards and certificates!

Try IXL free with 10 questions per day, and learn about how an IXL membership can boost learning even further. With an IXL account you'll get:

Limitless learning
Boost learning and curiosity with over 17,000 topics in math, English, science, social studies, and Spanish for everyone, from K-12.

Support and encouragement
Get instant feedback, step-by-step explanations, videos, and more! IXL makes it easy to learn from mistakes and feel good about it.

Awards and certificates
Whimsical awards and certificates celebrate your child's achievements and keep them motivated.

A unique plan for every child
IXL builds a growth path for your child by meeting them at their learning level and giving them exactly what they need to work on next.

The learning app families trust
In over 75 scientific research studies, IXL is proven to help students make bigger learning gains and build confidence in their abilities. No wonder it's used by 1 in 4 students across the U.S.!

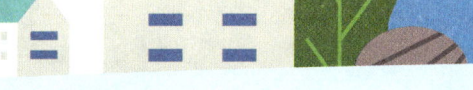

Ready to open up an exciting new world of learning?

Join hundreds of thousands of parents across the world and give your child access to unlimited learning with an IXL membership!

Learn more at ixl.com/summer-bridge/5-6

Skills Matrix

Day	Addition & Subtraction	Algebra	Capitalization & Punctuation	Critical Thinking	Data Analysis	Decimals, Fractions, & Percentages	Geometry & Measurement	Grammar	Language Arts	Multiplication & Division	Numbers	Parts of Speech	Problem Solving	Reading Comprehension	Science	Sentence Structure & Types	Social Studies	Vocabulary & Spelling	Writing
1	★									★								★	
2								★			★	★					★		
3								★	★					★					
4							★											★	★
5						★						★						★	
6						★						★		★				★	
7				★						★								★	★
8												★	★		★			★	
9								★		★				★					
10										★		★							
11		★								★								★	
12							★					★						★	★
13		★					★					★		★					
14				★										★				★	★
15					★				★									★	
16								★				★		★				★	
17									★			★	★					★	
18												★	★		★			★	
19						★						★		★					
20			★			★				★								★	
					★			BONUS PAGES!							★		★	★	★
1			★			★								★				★	
2						★								★				★	
3						★						★					★	★	
4						★		★				★							
5						★	★							★					
6						★					★	★							★
7					★													★	★
8								★	★					★					
9							★		★									★	
10					★			★		★					★				
11	★							★		★				★					

Skills Matrix

Day	Addition & Subtraction	Algebra	Capitalization & Punctuation	Critical Thinking	Data Analysis	Decimals, Fractions, & Percentages	Geometry & Measurement	Grammar	Language Arts	Multiplication & Division	Numbers	Parts of Speech	Problem Solving	Reading Comprehension	Science	Sentence Structure & Types	Social Studies	Vocabulary & Spelling	Writing
12		★							★	★									★
13		★						★	★	★									
14										★				★		★			
15			★						★			★		★					
16		★					★				★			★					
17										★				★					
18						★			★							★		★	
19									★	★									★
20		★												★				★	
					★	★	★	BONUS PAGES!						★		★			
1							★	★			★			★					
2								★		★	★			★					★
3					★									★				★	
4		★													★			★	
5		★			★													★	
6						★							★	★					
7							★		★										
8							★							★					
9			★				★							★					
10							★		★						★				★
11			★			★											★	★	
12						★								★				★	
13					★													★	
14					★									★	★	★			
15					★									★		★			
16			★				★		★					★				★	
17									★		★					★			
18					★								★	★					
19							★		★										★
20					★			★	★						★				
					★			BONUS PAGES! ★					★	★		★		★

Summer Reading and Free E-books

Reading is important all year, not just during school. This summer, set yourself a reading goal and challenge yourself to complete it. You can make your goal one book a month, or even one a week! Choose a goal realistic for you.

Give some of these summer reading ideas a try to make summer reading fun and meaningful.

Read in a New Place
Read in a hammock, under a shady tree, in a sunny spot, on a porch, in a park, in a fort, on a picnic blanket, at a playground, in a tent, or any other spot you've never read before.

Make a Reading List
Make a list of books in a genre you like, books with characters your age, books by your favorite author, or come up with your own list theme. Read as many as you can and check them off as you do.

Read a Summer Book
Choose a book that is summer themed. It could be about a summer trip, summer vacation, a new neighbor, a fun adventure, or set at the beach or in a tropical location.

Be a Chef
Read a cookbook or a book about food. Choose a recipe in the book to make. Write it on a recipe card. Then make it (and enjoy it)! It's up to you if you share it!

Check Your Library
Sign up for your local library's summer reading challenge (or find one online to participate in).

Start a Book Club
Join (or start) a book club with friends or family members. Take turns choosing the book.

Free E-books!

Get started on summer reading fun now by scanning the QR codes for free e-books!

The Evolution of Food

Mythical Monsters

People Power

Plants That Break the Rules

© Carson Dellosa Education

SUMMER READING LOG

DATE	TITLE	Minutes Read	# OF PAGES

SECTION 1

Monthly Goals

A goal is something that you want to accomplish and must work toward. Sometimes, reaching a goal can be difficult.

Think of three goals to set for yourself this month. For example, you may want to exercise for 30 minutes each day. Write your goals on the lines. Post them someplace where you will see them every day.

Draw a line through each goal as you meet it. Feel proud that you have met your goals and set new ones to continue to challenge yourself.

1. _____
2. _____
3. _____

Word List

The following words are used in this section. Use a dictionary to look up each word that you do not know. Write three sentences. Use a word from the word list in each sentence.

biome   physician
collide   porous
famished   sensible
fragile   slogan
geyser   superb

1. _____
   _____
2. _____
   _____
3. _____
   _____

Introduction to Flexibility

This section includes Let's Play Today and Mindful Moments activities that focus on flexibility. These activities are designed to help you become flexible physically and mentally. If you have limited mobility, feel free to modify any suggested activity or choose a different one from the list on the following page.

When we talk about flexibility with regard to our bodies, we are referring to how easily our bodies move. If our body isn't flexible, then we will have trouble doing everyday tasks, such as tying our shoes, reaching for things, or playing games or sports.

Over the summer, make a point to stretch regularly to keep your arms and legs moving easily and your back from getting sore. Challenge yourself to touch your toes daily. Did you know that everyday activities like reaching for a dropped pencil can practice stretching?

Mental flexibility is just as important as physical flexibility. Being mentally flexible means being open-minded. We all know how disappointing it can be when things do not go the way we want them to. Having a fun day at the park ruined because of rain is frustrating. Feeling disappointed or angry as a reaction is normal. In life, there will be situations where unexpected things happen. Often, it is how someone reacts to those circumstances that affects the outcome. It is important to have realistic expectations, brainstorm solutions to improve a disappointing situation, or look on the bright side of a disappointment to find joy even when things do not go as planned.

You can show flexibility of character and mind by being understanding, respecting others' differences, sharing, taking turns, and more. Learning to be flexible now at your age will give you the ability to handle unexpected situations in the years to come.

Engaging Online Practice

Bring learning to life with fun, interactive activities on IXL! Look for the Skill ID box and type the 3-digit code into the search bar on IXL.com or the IXL mobile app. Ten questions per day are free!

Skill IDs: 5UN • D9K

© Carson Dellosa Education

SECTION 1

Let's Play Today

Get up and moving with these Let's Play Today activities. Section 1 focuses on flexibility. Flexibility helps your body move in its full range of motion and helps you avoid injuring yourself when exercising or playing. Use this list in addition to or as a replacement for any Let's Play Today suggestions on the activity pages. This list was developed to be inclusive of a variety of abilities. Choose the ones that are a good fit for you! Make modifications as needed. These activities may require adult supervision. See page 2 for full caution information.

Bouncy Ball Back-and-Forth:
In an open outdoor space, kick or toss a large bouncy ball back and forth with a friend, family member, or neighbor. Stretch your legs when you kick the ball or lunge to stop a returning ball. Stretch your arms if you are catching it.

The Shallow End Hop:
In the shallow end of a pool, stand on one leg and hold your arms out to your side. Hop from one side of the pool to the other without using your other leg. Switch legs and hop back to the other side.

Stretch to Pop:
Grab a container of bubbles and head outside. Blow bubbles high into the air. Stretch your arms and legs to reach them and pop them before they fall back toward the ground.

Walk a Tightrope:
Use a piece of sidewalk chalk or tape to make a long, thin line on the cement outside. Putting one foot in front of the other and with arms stretched out to the side, slowly walk on the line until you come to the end, being careful to keep your balance. Then turn around and walk back the other way. Try not to step off the line.

Weaving In and Out:
In a yard or at a playground, set up an obstacle course that is made up of traffic cones, toys, or other objects. Start with the objects spread out pretty far, and then move them closer together to make it a little more difficult. Try to move through it without touching any of the objects.

Add., Subt., Mult., & Div./Vocabulary

Solve each problem.

1. 793 × 27 = _____
2. 483 × 175 = _____
3. 7,136 ÷ 8 = _____
4. 763,947 − 244,398 = _____
5. 8)9,696 = _____
6. 45)2,974 = _____
7. 63,459 − 21,365 = _____
8. $678.14 + $990.27 = _____

Circle the definition of the underlined word as it is used in the sentence.

9. Alexi was <u>upset</u> about her score on the spelling test.

    A. spilled or overturned   **B.** distressed or anxious

10. Place a cool <u>compress</u> on your head if you have a headache.

    A. a cloth pad   **B.** push together

11. Do you use vanilla <u>extract</u> in your pancake batter?

    A. take out   **B.** concentrated form

12. The <u>proceeds</u> from the bake sale will go toward our class field trip to a living history farm.

    A. money from a sale   **B.** moves forward

Mindful Moment

Stand tall like a tree, arms stretched straight above your head. Take in a deep breath, hold it, then slowly release it. Do this 5 times.

DAY 1

Vocabulary/Add., Subt., Mult., & Div.

Add a prefix to each base word to make a new word. Use *mis-*, *re-*, *un-*, *non-*, or *pre-*.

13. name _____rename_____
14. read _____
15. heat _____
16. sure _____
17. treat _____
18. fit _____
19. turn _____
20. call _____
21. stop _____
22. place _____

Find the value of each expression.

23. (4 + 8) × 10 = _____
24. 45 ÷ (6 − 3) = _____
25. 46 − [(24 ÷ 6) + 19] = _____
26. (18 ÷ 2) × (56 ÷ 7) = _____
27. (3 × 14) ÷ 7 = _____
28. [(14 + 12) × 2] ÷ 13 = _____
29. 125 − (5 × 12) = _____
30. (15 × 4) × (8 − 3) = _____
31. 16 × [2 + (18 ÷ 3)] = _____
32. 13 + (84 ÷ 2) − (55 ÷ 11) = _____

Numbers/Parts of Speech

Skill IDs: BLQ • 2NZ

DAY 2

Write each expanded number in standard form.

1. $(2 \times 1{,}000{,}000) + (6 \times 100{,}000) + (8 \times 10{,}000) + (5 \times 1{,}000) + (3 \times 100) + (2 \times 10) + (2 \times 1) =$

   _____

2. $(4 \times 100) + (7 \times 10) + (8 \times 1) + (5 \times \frac{1}{10}) + (3 \times \frac{1}{100}) =$

   _____

3. $(2 \times 10{,}000{,}000) + (3 \times 1{,}000{,}000) + (4 \times 100{,}000) + (9 \times 1{,}000) + (3 \times 10) + (6 \times 1) =$

   _____

4. $(2 \times 1{,}000) + (1 \times 100) + (1 \times 10) + (1 \times 1) + (9 \times \frac{1}{100}) + (7 \times \frac{1}{1{,}000}) =$

   _____

Write each standard number in expanded form.

5. 37,126,489.2 _____

   _____

6. 2,069.044 _____

   _____

Circle the prepositions in each sentence.

7. Jada and Helen had not seen each other for 50 years.

8. "Tell me about Grandpa," said Randy.

9. They carried the water packs on their backs.

10. I would go into the garden, but it is muddy.

11. Tomas passed the peas to his mother.

12. We should meet somewhere beyond the city limits.

13. The lights activate automatically after sunset.

14. Please put an umbrella in the trunk.

15

Circle the word that correctly completes each sentence.

15. One day, Wendy and Jamal decided to go (camp, camping, camped).

16. They (pack, packing, packed) everything they needed in their truck.

17. Then, they went to (hunt, hunting, hunted) for a good place to camp.

18. After looking for a long time, they (pick, picking, picked) a great campsite.

19. (Park, Parking, Parked) the truck was tricky because the ground was slippery.

20. Wendy went (splash, splashing, splashed) through a big puddle.

Use an atlas or online map to find the major North American city that is closest to each latitude and longitude.

21. 61°N, 150°W _____
22. 34°N, 118°W _____
23. 39°N, 95°W _____
24. 30°N, 90°W _____
25. 42°N, 83°W _____
26. 45°N, 76°W _____
27. 35°N, 107°W _____
28. 41°N, 74°W _____
29. 40°N, 83°W _____
30. 51°N, 114°W _____

Grammar/Language Arts

DAY 3

Correct the subject/verb agreement errors in the paragraph. Cross off the incorrect word and write the correct word above it.

Every Monday, students in Mrs. Verdan's class works with partners to complete math challenges. Each pair select its own work space. Jeremy and Melvin goes to the math center. Maria and Lea likes the sunny table by the window. Hector and Jeff chooses chairs near the board. All of the pairs has 45 minutes to solve the day's puzzle. Most of them finishes on time. They shares their solutions with the whole group. A few students meets with Mrs. Verdan after school. Mrs. Verdan's students always enjoys the weekly math challenges.

Complete each proverb with a word from the word bank. Then, explain what the proverb means.

| leap | cake | turn | spice | basket |

1. Variety is the _____ of life.
   _____

2. You cannot have your _____ and eat it too.
   _____

3. Don't put all your eggs in one _____.
   _____

4. Look before you _____.
   _____

5. One good _____ deserves another.
   _____

DAY 3

Reading Comprehension

Read the passage. Then, answer the questions.

The Eagle Has Landed

On July 20, 1969, at 1:45 P.M., American astronauts Neil Armstrong and Buzz Aldrin detached their Lunar Module (LM) from the *Apollo 11* spacecraft to head toward the moon. "The Eagle has wings," Armstrong stated. At 3:46 P.M., the LM emerged from behind the moon. It was at an altitude of about 20 miles (32.2 km) from the moon. The astronauts had to make the all-important decision of whether to remain in orbit or to descend to the lunar surface. This might be their only chance to land on the moon.

At approximately 4:07 P.M., Armstrong pressed the button marked "Proceed." But, the computer-controlled guidance system was about to take Aldrin and Armstrong into a football field-sized crater filled with big boulders and rocks. With only precious seconds to spare, Armstrong took manual control of the spacecraft. He found a clear area amid the menacing rock field below. "Houston," Armstrong radioed. "Tranquility base here. The Eagle has landed."

Armstrong was the first human to set foot on the moon. As his left foot touched the lunar surface to take the first step, he spoke the now famous words, "That's one small step for [a] man, one giant leap for mankind."

6. What was Armstrong referring to when he said, "The Eagle has landed"?
   _____

7. The word *lunar* is used several times in the passage. What is another word for *lunar*?
   _____

8. Why does the author call the decision to land on the moon an "all-important decision"?
   _____

9. What was the significance of this mission to humankind?
   _____

10. What does this passage tell you about the type of people Armstrong and Aldrin were when they made this journey?
    _____

Let's Play Today * See page 12.

Set up laundry baskets, buckets, or other objects at varying lengths from where you're standing and toss balls into them.

© Carson Dellosa Education

Geometry/Vocabulary

Identify each figure using letters from the box. All but one figure will be identified by more than one word.

A. regular polygon	**B.** triangle	**C.** rhombus	**D.** kite
E. quadrilateral	**F.** parallelogram	**G.** hexagon	**H.** rectangle
	I. square	**J.** trapezoid	

1.
_____

2.
_____

3.
_____

4.
_____

5.
_____

6.
_____

7.
_____

8.
_____

Circle a word to match each description. Underline its root.

9. Which word contains a Greek root that means "earth"?
   spectacle   automobile   geography

10. Which word contains a Latin root that means "carry"?
    prediction   transportation   inspect

11. Which word contains a Latin root that means "drag or pull"?
    inject   tripod   extract

12. Which word contains a Greek root that means "the study of"?
    meteorology   structure   telegraph

Vocabulary/Writing

Add a prefix, suffix, or both to each base word. Write the meaning of the new word on the line. With an adult, use the Internet to find more prefixes and suffixes if needed.

Common Prefixes:	Common Suffixes:
anti-, mis-, dis-, un-	-ment, -able, -ous, -less

13. _____ agree _____ _____

14. _____ placed _____

15. _____ respect _____ _____

16. _____ capable _____

17. avoid _____ _____

18. _____ change _____

19. delay _____ _____

20. _____ number _____ _____

21. loyal _____ _____

22. hazard _____ _____

23. care _____ _____

24. _____ depend _____ _____

A limerick is a humorous five-line poem with a set rhyme scheme: AABBA. This means that the first, second, and fifth lines rhyme and the third and fourth lines rhyme. Write a limerick about your summer vacation.

_____

_____

_____

_____

> There once was a fly on the wall,
> I wonder, why didn't it fall?
> Because its feet stuck?
> Or was it just luck?
> Or does gravity miss things so small?

Geometry/Vocabulary

Identify each figure using letters from the box. All but one figure will be identified by more than one word.

A. regular polygon	B. triangle	C. rhombus	D. kite
E. quadrilateral	F. parallelogram	G. hexagon	H. rectangle
	I. square	J. trapezoid	

1.
_____

2.
_____

3.
_____

4.
_____

5.
_____

6.
_____

7.
_____

8.
_____

Circle a word to match each description. Underline its root.

9. Which word contains a Greek root that means "earth"?
   spectacle   automobile   geography

10. Which word contains a Latin root that means "carry"?
    prediction   transportation   inspect

11. Which word contains a Latin root that means "drag or pull"?
    inject   tripod   extract

12. Which word contains a Greek root that means "the study of"?
    meteorology   structure   telegraph

© Carson Dellosa Education

DAY 4

Vocabulary/Writing

Add a prefix, suffix, or both to each base word. Write the meaning of the new word on the line. With an adult, use the Internet to find more prefixes and suffixes if needed.

Common Prefixes: anti-, mis-, dis-, un-

Common Suffixes: -ment, -able, -ous, -less

13. _____ agree _____ _____

14. _____ placed _____

15. _____ respect _____ _____

16. _____ capable _____

17. avoid _____ _____

18. _____ change _____

19. delay _____ _____

20. _____ number _____ _____

21. loyal _____ _____

22. hazard _____ _____

23. care _____ _____

24. _____ depend _____ _____

A limerick is a humorous five-line poem with a set rhyme scheme: AABBA. This means that the first, second, and fifth lines rhyme and the third and fourth lines rhyme. Write a limerick about your summer vacation.

_____

_____

_____

_____

_____

> There once was a fly on the wall,
> I wonder, why didn't it fall?
> Because its feet stuck?
> Or was it just luck?
> Or does gravity miss things so small?

Decimals/Parts of Speech

Skill IDs: X8U • 7QW

DAY 5

Write the digit in the place named.

1. 325,251.58 _____
   thousands

2. 1,547.489 _____
   thousandths

3. 348,019.57 _____
   ten thousands

4. 10,825.643 _____
   tenths

5. 241,389,613 _____
   hundred millions

6. 12,541,698.489 _____
   hundredths

Correlative conjunctions join similar words, phrases, or clauses. Circle the correlative conjunctions in each sentence.

7. Last night, both Dion and Noreen won awards.

8. Just as cars follow street signs, so must bikes.

9. Neither the map nor the itinerary fit in Ophelia's scrapbook.

10. We could use either molasses or sugar to sweeten the cookies.

11. Bea not only decorated the cupcakes but also made them from scratch.

12. Neither Carlos nor Mirabel is going to the meeting tonight.

13. Either a period or a semicolon can correct a run-on sentence.

14. Whether it rains or not, we will play soccer.

Fast Fun Fact

Light travels so fast, it can cover 670 million miles in just an hour!

Vocabulary

Look at the meanings of the prefixes and suffixes. Use them to write the meaning of each word below.

Prefixes		Suffixes	
re-	back or again	-ment	the act, result, or product of
dis-	away, apart, or the opposite of	-ish	of or belonging to; like or about
un-	opposite, not, or lack of	-less	without or not
pre-	before		

15. punishment _____

16. disappear _____

17. presoak _____

18. rewind _____

19. colorless _____

20. precooked _____

21. unsure _____

22. brownish _____

Draw a line from a phrase on the left to a phrase on the right to complete a sentence.

23. The vibration of the loud music   ask someone you can trust.

24. If you want an honest opinion,   as the sea became rough.

25. Some students grasped the concept,   made the car thump.

26. A large glacier broke apart   while others were confused.

Fractions/Parts of Speech

Solve. Write answers in simplest form.

1. $5\frac{3}{8} + 2\frac{1}{4} =$ _____

2. $3\frac{5}{12} + \frac{2}{3} =$ _____

3. $4\frac{1}{3} - 1\frac{1}{7} =$ _____

4. $2\frac{1}{3} - \frac{5}{6} =$ _____

5. $\frac{4}{5} \times 1\frac{2}{3} =$ _____

6. $2\frac{1}{7} \times 3\frac{1}{2} =$ _____

7. $12 \div \frac{1}{8} =$ _____

8. $\frac{1}{9} \div 4 =$ _____

Combine each pair of sentences using a coordinating conjunction from the word bank. In compound sentences, use a comma before the coordinating conjunction.

| and | but | for | or | so | yet |

9. Dante went swimming in the pool. He did not go swimming in the lake.

_____

_____

10. She enjoys making art. She chooses to spend more time playing sports.

_____

_____

11. Josie picked up her backpack. She got on the bus.

_____

_____

12. We can watch the movie. We can meet Joe at the park.

_____

_____

Biomes of Canada

Canada has many different **biomes**, or areas with similar ecosystems. Some of the southern provinces are covered in grasslands. The Hudson Plains, near Hudson Bay, contain one-quarter of Earth's wetlands, which attract many migrating birds. Much of southern Canada is covered by the Boreal Shield, which includes forests and rivers that were once used for fur trade. Far northern Canada is covered by tundra, which contains permanently frozen ground called *permafrost*. Much of western Canada is within a mountain biome. The far southeastern provinces are in the Atlantic Maritime biome. *Maritime* refers to the sea. This area receives heavy rainfall because it is near the Atlantic Ocean. Along Canada's border with Alaska lie temperate rainforests. Because this area is near the Pacific Ocean, its climate is very mild. The smallest biome, a temperate deciduous forest, contains half of Canada's population and the cities of Toronto and Montreal.

13. What is the main idea of this paragraph?

    A. Some biomes are mountainous, and others have grasslands.

    B. Many people live in Toronto and Montreal.

    C. Canada has a variety of climates and landscapes.

14. What is a biome? _____

15. Name three biomes that can be found in Canada. _____
    _____

16. What is permanently frozen ground called? _____

17. Why does the Atlantic Maritime biome have heavy rainfall? _____
    _____

18. Which area in Canada contains one-quarter of Earth's wetlands?
    _____

19. What does the term *maritime* refer to? _____

Mindful Moment

How are you feeling today? Are you happy, anxious, sad? Think about how you feel and why you're feeling this way.

Division/Writing

DAY 7

Find each quotient. Round answers to the nearest thousandth.

1. 8)231
2. 5)3,305
3. 75)9,283
4. 4)394

5. 75)675
6. 40)7,384
7. 9)894
8. 70)5,824

Write a review of a book you have read. Support your opinion with reasons. Then, visit an online bookstore with an adult. Look up the book you reviewed and read reviews that others have written. How does your opinion of the book compare to others' opinions?

_____
_____
_____
_____
_____
_____
_____
_____
_____

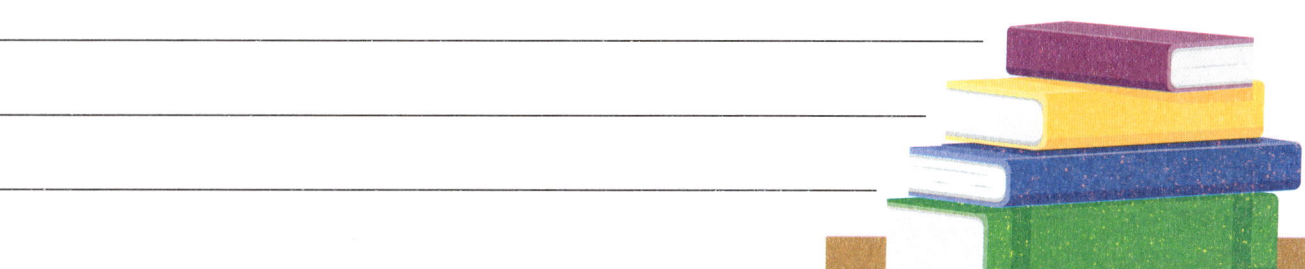

Write the letter of each definition next to the correct word.

9. ___G___ geyser

10. ___C___ generate

11. ___H___ slogan

12. ___B___ infuriate

13. ___D___ regulate

14. ___F___ collide

15. ___E___ ordeal

16. ___A___ sparse

A. not dense
B. to make angry
C. produce
D. control
E. a trying experience
F. make hard contact
G. hot spring
H. motto

The ages of these trees are 18 years, 27 years, 45 years, and 48 years. Use the clues and the table below to find and mark the age of each tree.

- The maple tree is planted beside the oldest tree.
- The pine tree is not the youngest tree.
- The oldest tree has the shortest name.
- The youngest tree is planted across from the maple tree.
- The second youngest tree never has leaves.

	18 years	27 years	45 years	48 years
17. Maple			X	
18. Pine		X		
19. Birch	X			
20. Oak				X

Problem Solving/Parts of Speech

Solve each problem. Write answers in simplest form.

1. Rupa picked $8\frac{1}{5}$ pounds of apples. Louisa picked $9\frac{2}{3}$ pounds of apples. How many more pounds of apples did Louisa pick than Rupa?

   _____ pounds

2. Tabitha is $4\frac{7}{12}$ feet tall. Her grandpa is $1\frac{4}{7}$ feet taller. How tall is Tabitha's grandpa?

   _____ feet tall

3. Ben watched a play. The first act was $\frac{5}{6}$ hours long. The intermission was $\frac{1}{4}$ hour long. The second act was $1\frac{1}{5}$ hours long. How long was Ben at the play altogether?

   _____ hours

4. Marcus watched a soccer match for $2\frac{1}{5}$ hours. Danica watched a football game for $3\frac{3}{8}$ hours. How much longer was the football game than the soccer match?

   _____ hours

Circle the action verbs. Underline the linking verbs.

walk	seem	is	cry	became
sound	wore	sneezed	become	blew
call	being	read	built	clapping
dance	will	eat	have been	watched
are	gather	cheer	was	chews
be	were	am	speak	have

Let's Play Today *See page 12.

Do a crab walk through an obstacle course you've created with cones, chairs, and other objects in your home.

Vocabulary/Science

Write a word from the word bank to complete each sentence.

| allergies | conduct | inlets | stethoscope |
| suspicious | knead | margin | owes |

5. The doctor listened to my heart through the _____.

6. The night watchman became _____ of the parked car.

7. Did you leave a _____ on each side of your paper?

8. Ted always _____ someone money.

9. Use both hands when you _____ the bread dough.

10. Three of my classmates have food _____.

11. Toby's _____ at the recital was extremely good.

12. All of the _____ around the lake were crowded with boats.

Matter exists in three states: solid, liquid, and gas. Write each word from the word bank under the correct heading.

air	box	dust
helium	hydrogen	ice
juice	lava	milk
oxygen	rock	water

Solid | Liquid | Gas

Multiplication/Grammar

Use mental math to find each product.

1. 0.07 × 10 = _____
2. 16 × 10 = _____
3. 50 × 0.50 = _____
4. 7 × 600 = _____
5. 5 × 900 = _____
6. 70 × 0.06 = _____
7. 30 × 400 = _____
8. 0.9 × 3,000 = _____
9. 30 × 5,000 = _____

Circle the form of the verb *to be* that correctly completes each sentence.

10. I (be, am) guessing the number of pennies in the jar.
11. What (is, be) your favorite month?
12. The workers (been, were) repairing the road in front of our house.
13. Uncle Caleb (was, were) laughing very loudly.
14. (Is, Are) you the team leader?
15. Carla (been, has been, have been) an astronaut for many years.
16. The old house (is being, are being) torn down.
17. We (be, will be) playing in the orchestra on Saturday night.

Write a sentence using each form of the verb *to be*. Make sure that your sentences are different from the ones above.

18. were _____
19. has been _____
20. was being _____

Search for this skill ID on IXL.com for more practice!

Reading Comprehension

Read the passage. Then, answer the questions.

The Lost Colony

Englishman Sir Walter Raleigh wanted to start a colony in the New World (North America). In 1585, Raleigh sent colonists to what is now North Carolina. The colonists did not want to work. They almost starved to death. They were taken back to England. Two years later, a second group of colonists sailed to the same place. They worked very hard to survive.

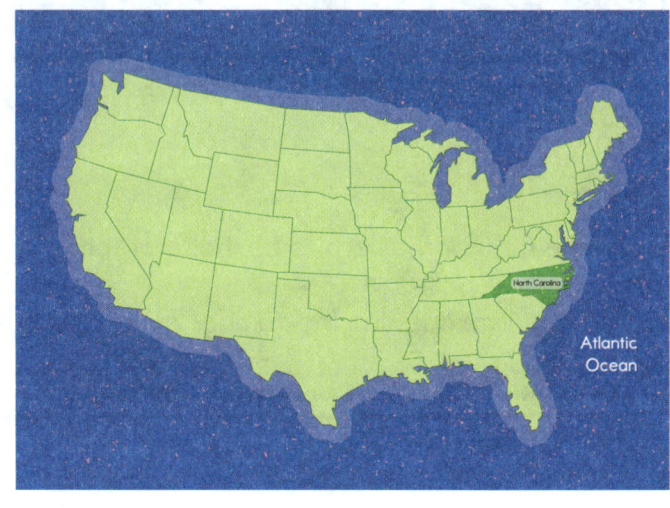

Because of a war involving England, Raleigh lost track of the colonists. In 1591, a ship from England arrived to check on the colonists, but the colonists had disappeared! There was no sign of life. All that the sailors found were some empty trunks, rotted maps, and the word CROATAN carved on the door post of the fort. Croatan was an island 100 miles south of the Lost Colony. No one knows whether the colonists were attacked by the Indigenous people of Croatan or whether the colonists went to live on Croatan Island. The Lost Colony has been a great mystery in American history.

21. Where is the Lost Colony? _____

22. How many years did it take Sir Walter Raleigh to send a ship to check on the second group of colonists? _____

23. Why do you think this colony was called the *Lost Colony*? _____

_____

24. Find another account of the Lost Colony online. How is it different from the passage above? Is it told from a different point of view? Explain below.

_____

_____

_____

_____

Multiplication/Parts of Speech

Day 10

Find each product.

1. 826 × 47
2. 584 × 29
3. 249 × 63
4. 973 × 51

5. 628 × 274
6. 831 × 347
7. 609 × 149
8. 586 × 781

Write the past-tense form of each irregular verb in parentheses to complete each sentence.

9. I (wear) _____wore_____ an old coat to school.

10. The telephone (ring) _____ 10 times before she answered it.

11. We each (choose) _____ a friend to go with us to Funland.

12. My brother (spend) _____ all of his allowance on ice cream.

13. I (awake) _____ when my dog jumped on my bed.

14. They (become) _____ excited when their team scored a point.

15. My uncle (bring) _____ me a T-shirt from his trip.

16. My friend (draw) _____ a picture of me.

17. The starfish (grow) _____ a new arm.

Parts of Speech

An interjection is a word or phrase that shows surprise or emotion. Underline each interjection and the punctuation following it.

18. OK, I understand this now.

19. Shh! We're trying to get our work done.

20. Ouch, get off my foot!

21. I passed! Wow!

22. Mmmm, something smells delicious!

23. Really, would you do that for me?

24. That isn't very nice. Stop!

25. I'm almost finished, hold on.

An adverb phrase, which is a type of prepositional phrase, usually describes how, when, or where something happened. Underline the adverb phrase in each sentence.

26. He could hear the crickets from the patio.

27. For 30 minutes she watched the parade go by.

28. Ava sang the song with a lot of emotion.

29. Without listening to directions, the kids started the scavenger hunt.

30. Behind the refrigerator, Lana's dad found a lot of dog fur.

 **Fast Fun Fact**
Some tortoises can live to be over 150 years old!

Multiplication/Parts of Speech

Estimate the amount of time it will take you to complete the 32 multiplication problems. Time yourself as you find the products.

Estimated Time: _____ Actual Time: _____ Number Correct: _____

1. 6 × 7 = _____
2. 8 × 9 = _____
3. 5 × 5 = _____
4. 11 × 5 = _____
5. 12 × 2 = _____
6. 6 × 9 = _____
7. 9 × 0 = _____
8. 9 × 6 = _____
9. 5 × 10 = _____
10. 11 × 10 = _____
11. 9 × 3 = _____
12. 9 × 12 = _____
13. 12 × 3 = _____
14. 10 × 9 = _____
15. 7 × 4 = _____
16. 6 × 8 = _____
17. 7 × 8 = _____
18. 9 × 11 = _____
19. 12 × 4 = _____
20. 7 × 10 = _____
21. 11 × 12 = _____
22. 7 × 3 = _____
23. 9 × 9 = _____
24. 5 × 11 = _____
25. 7 × 5 = _____
26. 12 × 10 = _____
27. 7 × 9 = _____
28. 10 × 10 = _____
29. 11 × 2 = _____
30. 12 × 6 = _____
31. 8 × 5 = _____
32. 6 × 11 = _____

Write the past-tense form of each irregular verb in parentheses to complete each sentence.

33. Kai (hold) _____ his breath for one minute.

34. My nose (bleed) _____ for five minutes last night.

35. The students (write) _____ essays telling what they did on their field trip.

36. Alexander (ride) _____ his Shetland pony in the parade last summer.

37. Julie's mother (teach) _____ us how to jump double Dutch.

38. The rain (freeze) _____ when it hit the pavement.

© Carson Dellosa Education

DAY 11

Algebra/Vocabulary

Write the expression for each phrase.

39. 16 more than the quotient of 84 and 12 _____

40. 14 less than the product of 12 and 7 _____

41. the quotient of 63 and 9 multiplied by 7 _____

42. the difference of 54 and 32 multiplied by the difference of 8 and 5

_____

43. $\frac{1}{3}$ of 36 multiplied by the difference of 15 and 2

_____

Choose the word or phrase from the word bank that has almost the same meaning as the underlined word or phrase in each sentence.

| cash crops | indigo |
| plantations | removed |

44. Indigenous people were <u>displaced</u> from their land. _____

45. Many Southern farmers grew <u>crops to sell for money</u>. _____

46. In 1744, Eliza Lucas developed <u>a blue dye made from a plant</u>. _____

47. The South had many <u>large farms where crops were grown and picked by enslaved people</u>. _____

Mindful Moment

Go outside and use your sense of sight to notice the nature around you (trees, flowers, snow, bugs). Give some thought to the beauty and wonder of nature.

Measurement/Parts of Speech

Find the volume of each cube.

1.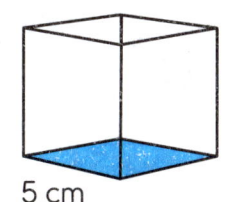
5 cm

V = _____

2.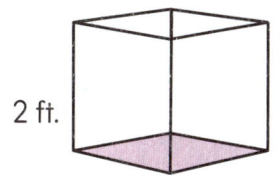
2 ft.

V = _____

3.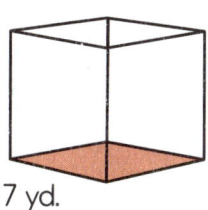
7 yd.

V = _____

4.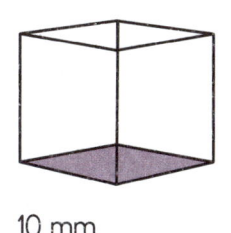
10 mm

V = _____

5.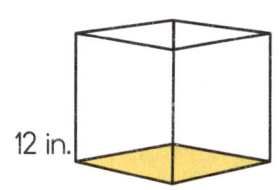
12 in.

V = _____

6.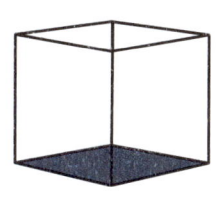
1 m

V = _____

To show the past tense of an irregular verb, change the spelling. The past participle is usually formed by adding a helping verb to the verb form that typically ends in -ed, -d, -t, -en, or -n. Write each irregular verb under the correct heading.

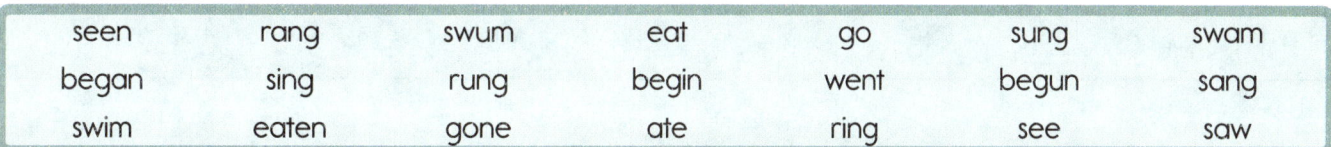

seen   rang   swum   eat   go   sung   swam
began   sing   rung   begin   went   begun   sang
swim   eaten   gone   ate   ring   see   saw

7. Present
   tear
   _____
   _____
   _____
   _____
   _____

8. Past
   tore
   _____
   _____
   _____
   _____
   _____

9. Past Participle
   has/have torn
   _____
   _____
   _____
   _____
   _____

DAY 12

Spelling/Writing

Circle the word that is misspelled in each row and spell it correctly on the line. Use a dictionary if you need help.

10.	refund	remodle	decode	preview	_____
11.	deposet	pretend	deflate	pace	_____
12.	mold	respond	giggel	revise	_____
13.	fiction	shelfes	unsafe	equip	_____
14.	transfer	defend	truthful	penlty	_____
15.	prdict	decide	gossip	fragile	_____
16.	beware	precice	porches	capital	_____
17.	leashes	cipher	estamate	climax	_____
18.	month	friendly	wrench	businiss	_____
19.	jiant	rectangle	guest	greet	_____

Think of a new ice-cream flavor you want to invent. What is in it? What will you call it? Describe it in a way that makes people want to try it.

_____
_____
_____
_____
_____
_____

Algebra & Geometry/Parts of Speech

Use the rule to write the missing numbers. Then, write each coordinate pair (x, y) and plot the points on the coordinate plane. Draw a line through all the points.

Rule: $y = x + 2$

Point	x	y	(x, y)
A	1	3	(1, 3)
B	2	___	(___, ___)
C	3	___	(___, ___)
D	4	___	(___, ___)
E	5	___	(___, ___)
F	6	___	(___, ___)
G	7	___	(___, ___)

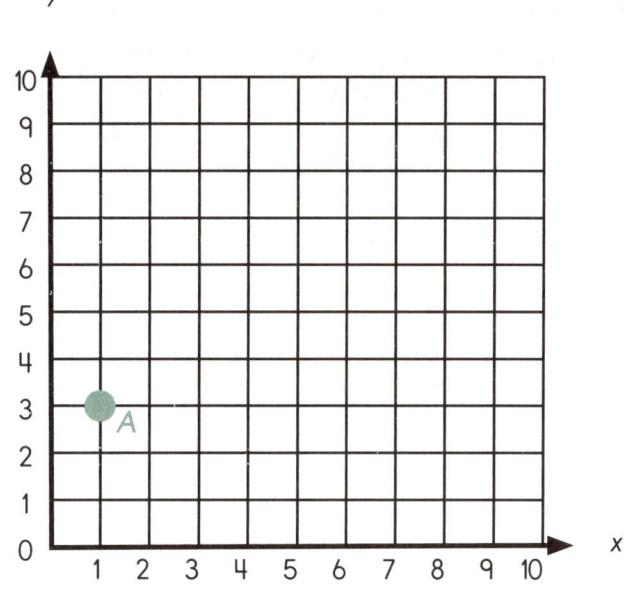

The future tense of a verb has the word *will* in front of the verb. Write the future-tense of each verb in parentheses to complete each sentence.

1. A group (build) _____ a huge rocket.

2. Technicians (check) _____ safety issues.

3. Ian and his dad (map) _____ the journey ahead of time.

4. Ian and his friends (board) _____ the rocket.

5. The announcer (count) _____ down to zero.

6. The rocket (launch) _____ into orbit.

7. The crew (view) _____ Earth from space.

8. They (observe) _____ comets and asteroids.

Let's Play Today *See page 12.

With your feet together on the ground, slowly bend over to try to touch your fingertips to your toes. Hold this stretch for 30 seconds.

Earth's History

Dinosaurs lived long ago—approximately 60 million years ago. Today, all that is left of them are their fossils, bones, and footprints. But, what does 60 million years mean to us? Scientists developed a geologic time scale that illustrates the periods in Earth's history. It can help those of us living today gain some perspective about the time involved in the development of life on Earth.

Read the chart. Then, answer the questions.

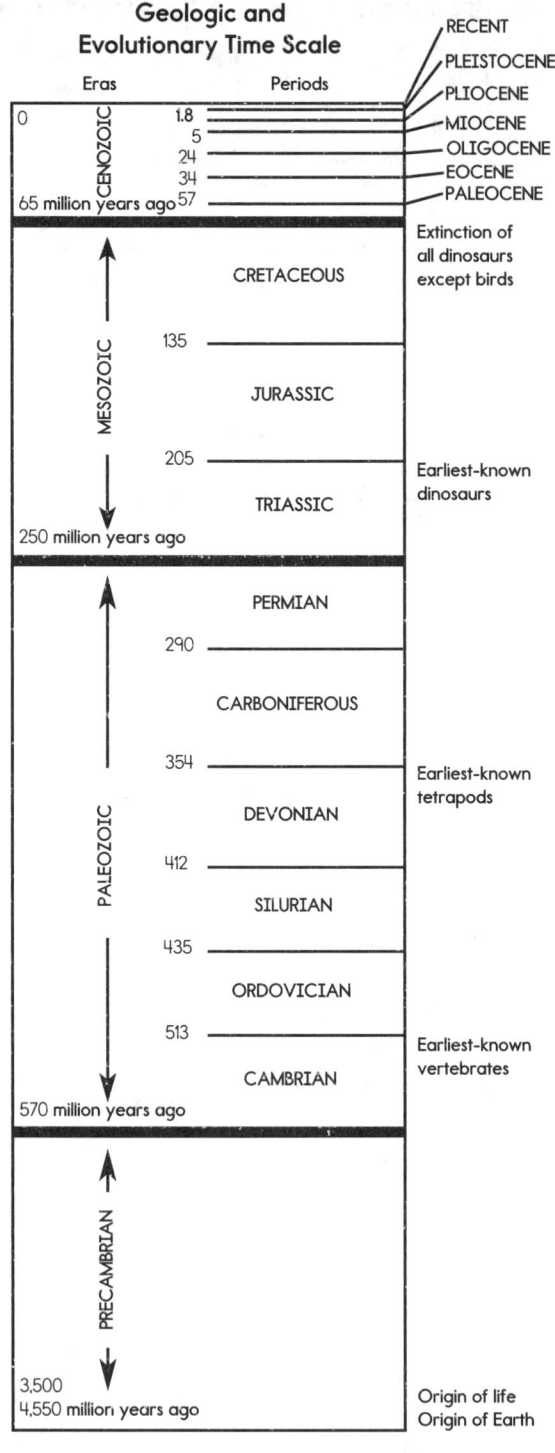

9. Earth's history is divided into how many major eras? _____

10. What are the names of the eras?
_____
_____
_____

11. In which era did dinosaurs exist?
_____

12. Into how many periods is the Mesozoic era divided?
_____

13. What are the Mesozoic periods' names?
_____
_____
_____

14. In which era do you live?
_____

Problem Solving/Punctuation

How Much Does a Dozen Eggs Weigh?

Small Eggs	Medium Eggs	Large Eggs	X-Large Eggs	Jumbo Eggs
18 oz.	21 oz.	24 oz.	27 oz.	30 oz.

Use the information above to answer each question.

1. Six dozen _____ eggs weigh a total of 180 ounces.

2. Which weighs more: 3 dozen jumbo eggs or 6 dozen small eggs?

   _____

3. If 5 dozen eggs weigh 120 ounces total, which size are they? _____

4. What is the minimum weight you can have if you have 4 dozen eggs?

   _____ ounces of _____ eggs

5. If you bought a dozen of each size of egg, what would be the total weight

   in ounces? _____

Titles of longer works, like books and movies, are italicized. Titles of shorter works, like songs and poems, are set in quotation marks. Punctuate the title in each sentence correctly, or underline titles that would be italicized in type.

6. This summer, I read a great book—Stargirl by Jerry Spinelli.

7. Grandma Cherice's favorite movie is The Wizard of Oz.

8. Amina borrowed Walk Two Moons and Wonder from the library.

9. The first song Keiko memorized for her role in the play Grease was Summer Nights.

10. What time does the next performance of Peter Pan begin?

11. Mariana sang The Wheels on the Bus to the little boys she was babysitting.

12. I'll never forget the first time I saw Star Wars.

13. Our whole family enjoys watching the show Fresh Off the Boat together.

DAY 14

Spelling/Writing

Correct the journal entry. Cross out each misspelled word and rewrite the word correctly above it.

Febuary 8, 2024

Dear Journel,

It has definately been a busy weekend. My calender was completely full. On Friday morning, I opened the door after the doorbell rang. I was expecting to see my friend and naybor, Adrienne. Instead, I saw Aunt Catrina. I was happy and suprised. There was not much time to talk. I had to leave for school in a few minutes, and Mom would head to the library in about an hour. "I took an early train," Aunt Catrina explained. "I know everyone will be gone all day. Don't worry about me. I will clean out the cuboards and vacume the living room while your gone. We will catch up tonight. I especialy look forward to the priviledge of talking to you." Then she gave me a big hug. We talked untill it was time to leave for school.

Write five questions that you would like to ask the leader of your country.

1. _____
2. _____
3. _____
4. _____
5. _____

Data Analysis/Language Arts

For a lab, Louis's science class is using 10 test tubes filled with different solutions. Louis used a line plot to show the liquid volume of each test tube. Use the data to answer the questions.

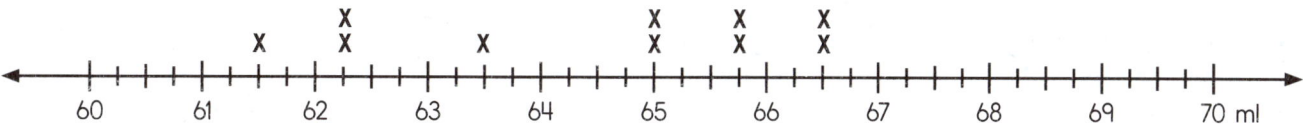

1. What is the total liquid volume of test tubes that contain less than 65 ml?

   _____

2. What is the total liquid volume of all 10 test tubes?

   _____

3. If the solutions from all 10 tubes were poured together and then redistributed evenly, how much liquid volume of solution would be in each test tube?

   _____

4. Louis wants to add water to the solutions so that each test tube contains 70 ml. How much water will he need for all 10?

   _____

The glossary below is from a kids' cookbook. Use it to answer the questions.

> **baste:** to brush a liquid, such as fat or drippings, over meat during roasting
> **blanch:** to immerse a fruit or vegetable in boiling water, remove it, and place it in a bowl of ice water
> **caramelize:** to brown sugar over medium heat
> **dilute:** to thin a liquid by adding more liquid, particularly milk or water
> **julienne:** to cut food into long, thin strips

5. Give an example of a food you might blanch. _____

6. If you added an entry for the word *dredge*, where would you place it?

   _____

7. Alysha cut carrots and cucumbers into long strips. What is another word for this?

   _____

8. Would you be more likely to baste a strawberry cake or a pot roast?

   _____

DAY 15

Vocabulary

Write a synonym for the word in parentheses to complete each sentence. Use a thesaurus if you need help.

9. I had to (finish) _____complete_____ my work before I could go with my friends.

10. Sarah and Angie go for a (walk) _____ every day except Sunday.

11. I cannot (find) _____ the information I need for my report.

12. You should write all of the important events of your (trip) _____ .

13. Will you please (show) _____ how your new invention works?

14. They will (try) _____ to climb Mount Everest again next summer.

15. The Hubble Space Telescope (completes) _____ one orbit around Earth every 96 minutes.

16. The value of this coin will (grow) _____ over the years.

Homophones are words that sound the same but have different meanings (and usually different spellings). Circle the correct homophone for each sentence.

17. We boarded the (plain, plane) just in time.

18. The (flower, flour) in the vase was wilting.

19. A king sits on a (thrown, throne).

20. The air freshener has a strong (scent, cent).

21. My sister stubbed her (toe, tow) on the table.

22. The plastic bag (blew, blue) out of the recycle bin.

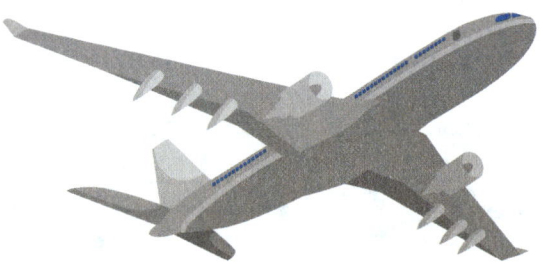

 **Fast Fun Fact**

The first bubble gum, which was invented in 1906, was called Blibber-Blubber!

Grammar/Parts of Speech

Circle the verb in parentheses that agrees with the subject of each sentence.

1. People (use, uses) various kinds of watercraft for fun.
2. Old-fashioned muscle power (propel, propels) some types of watercraft.
3. Some rafts (is, are) made by tying pieces of wood together.
4. Children often (enjoy, enjoys) canoeing at summer camps.
5. One paddler (steer, steers) a type of canoe called a kayak.
6. The paddle (is, are) double-bladed.

More than one adjective can be used to modify the same noun. Underline the adjectives in each sentence. Then, circle the words they modify.

7. The wild, eerie wind frightened the children.
8. A fuzzy brown caterpillar was creeping down the sidewalk.
9. Staci splashed some fresh, cool water on her face.
10. The hot, tired explorers swam in a large, clear lake.

Comparative adjectives compare two things. Superlative adjectives compare three or more things. Circle the correct comparative (-er) or superlative (-est) adjective for each sentence.

11. What is the (longer, longest) word in the English dictionary?
12. Our back door is (wider, widest) than our front door.
13. Mozart was one of the world's (younger, youngest) composers.
14. The gorilla is the (larger, largest) of all of the apes.
15. New Jersey is a (smaller, smallest) state than Pennsylvania.

Reading Comprehension

Read the paragraph. Then, answer the questions.

from *The Wind in the Willows* by Kenneth Grahame

The Mole had been working very hard all the morning, spring-cleaning his little home. First with brooms, then with dusters; then on ladders and steps and chairs, with a brush and a pail of whitewash; till he had dust in his throat and eyes, and splashes of whitewash all over his black fur, and an aching back and weary arms. Spring was moving in the air above and in the earth below and around him, **penetrating** even his dark and lowly little house with its spirit of divine discontent and longing. It was small wonder, then, that he suddenly flung down his brush on the floor, said 'Bother!' and 'O blow!' and also 'Hang spring-cleaning!' and bolted out of the house without even waiting to put on his coat. Something up above was calling him imperiously, and he made for the steep little tunnel which answered in his case to the gravelled carriage-drive owned by animals whose residences are nearer to the sun and air. So he scraped and scratched and scrabbled and scrooged and then he scrooged again and scrabbled and scratched and scraped, working busily with his little paws and muttering to himself, 'Up we go! Up we go!' till at last, pop! his snout came out into the sunlight, and he found himself rolling in the warm grass of a great meadow.

16. What does the word *penetrating* mean in the story?

_____

17. Find an example of alliteration in the paragraph and write it on the lines. How does it contribute to the story? _____

_____

_____

18. How does Grahame create the character of the Mole? What details help paint a picture of his personality? _____

_____

_____

Mindful Moment

Looking into a mirror, name something that you like about yourself. "I like . . ." Say it to yourself many times.

Problem Solving/Parts of Speech

Solve each problem. Write answers in simplest form.

1. Nola studied for her math test for $\frac{1}{4}$ hour in the morning, $1\frac{3}{8}$ hours after school, and $\frac{1}{2}$ hour before bed. How long did she study altogether?

   _____ hours

2. The grocer put $3\frac{1}{3}$ pounds of potatoes on the scale. Then they removed a potato weighing $\frac{4}{5}$ pound. How much weight is on the scale now?

   _____ pounds

3. A recipe calls for 2 cups of flour, $\frac{1}{4}$ cup of sugar, and $\frac{1}{3}$ cup of milk. What is the total volume of the three ingredients?

   _____ cups

4. The distance between two towns is $12\frac{5}{8}$ miles. Mr. Lang has driven $4\frac{5}{12}$ miles of the distance. How much farther does he have left to go?

   _____ miles

Write *PA* if the underlined word is a proper adjective. Write *PN* if the word is a proper noun.

5. _____ Many people from <u>Nigeria</u> have come to the United States to live.

6. _____ Years ago, many <u>Italian</u> immigrants landed in America.

7. _____ People came from <u>Ireland</u> in the 1800s and 1900s.

8. _____ Some <u>German</u> people immigrated to America too.

9. _____ Some of the first <u>English</u> colonists were the Puritans.

10. _____ They left <u>England</u> for several reasons in the 1600s.

11. _____ <u>Japanese</u> immigrants brought agricultural products such, as tea plants and bamboo roots, to the United States.

12. _____ <u>Chinese</u> immigration in the 1850s, fueled partly by the California gold rush, led to a hard life for immigrants.

Search for this skill ID on IXL.com for more practice!

Vocabulary/Language Arts

Complete the crossword puzzle with synonyms for the bold words. Use the word bank.

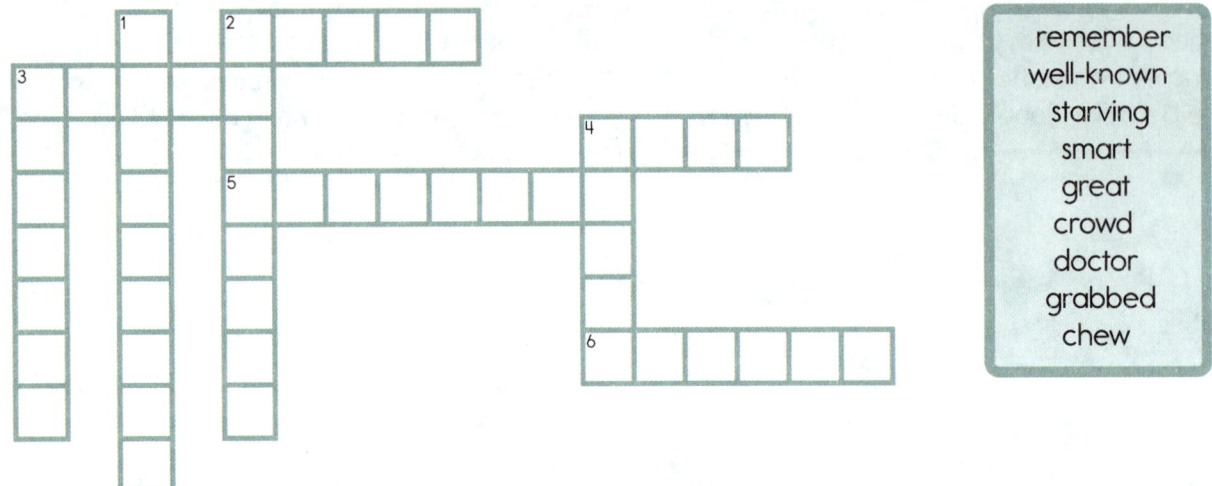

remember
well-known
starving
smart
great
crowd
doctor
grabbed
chew

Across

2. My **intelligent** dog learned a new trick.
3. Your party was **superb**!
4. Jack's puppy likes to **gnaw** on toys.
5. Do you **recall** the phone number?
6. I went to my **physician** when I got sick.

Down

1. On Monday, a **famous** artist will visit us.
2. I was **famished**, so I ate a snack.
3. My aunt **grasped** the railing as she came down the stairs.
4. A **mob** of fans was at the concert.

Below are some sentences about the first president of the United States, George Washington. Read the sentences and put them in the correct chronological order (1–7).

_____ When his father died in 1743, Washington went to live on a plantation known as Mount Vernon.

_____ George Washington was born in 1732 in Virginia.

_____ Washington married Martha Dandridge Custis in 1759.

_____ Washington became the first president of the United States in 1789.

_____ George Washington died in 1799.

_____ In 1758, Washington served in the Virginia House of Burgesses.

_____ Washington served in the French and Indian War from 1754–1758.

Problem Solving/Parts of Speech

DAY 18

Solve each problem. Write answers in simplest form.

1. A single serving of pasta salad requires $\frac{1}{4}$ cup of dry pasta. How much pasta is needed for $9\frac{1}{2}$ servings?

   _____ cups of dry pasta

2. Deepak stacked 14 copies of the same book. Each book is $1\frac{3}{8}$ inches thick. How high is the stack of books?

   _____ inches

3. Megan has 5 yards of cloth to make napkins. She needs $\frac{1}{8}$ yard for each napkin. How many napkins can Megan make with the cloth?

   _____ napkins

4. Trinity has 12 ounces of tea leaves. If each cup of tea requires $\frac{2}{3}$ ounce of tea leaves, how many cups of tea can Trinity make?

   _____ cups of tea

Adverbs are words that modify or describe verbs, adjectives, and other adverbs. Adverbs tell *how*, *when*, and *where*. Many adverbs end with *-ly*. Write each adverb next to the question it answers.

above	carefully	eagerly	far	hard	here
immediately	inside	lately	quickly	never	often
softly	soon	there	today	upstairs	wildly

5. When?						
6. How?						
7. Where?						

DAY 18

Vocabulary/Science

Read each pair of sentences. Circle the word in the first sentence that is the antonym for the bold word in the second sentence.

8. The air was moist and cool after the heavy rain last night.

    Once the sun was out for a couple of hours, the air seemed to be **dry**.

9. A lost dog was enclosed in a pen until the owner came to get it.

    When the dog was **released** to its owner, it jumped up to lick him.

10. Dad was ignorant about the driving laws when he visited England.

    He quickly became **knowledgeable** by reading a book of the rules.

Write a word or group of words from the word bank to complete each sentence.

center of Earth	core	outer core
lithosphere	inner core	mantle

11. The core of Earth has two parts. The _____ is liquid.

    The _____ is solid.

12. The _____ includes the crust and the uppermost mantle.

13. The _____ is the thickest layer and is extremely hot.

14. As the _____ is approached, pressure and temperature increase.

15. One reason that the crust and upper _____ are brittle is because they are the outermost and coldest layers of Earth.

Let's Play Today * See page 12.

With your feet shoulder-width apart, slowly reach up toward the stars with your left arm. Bring your arm down, then repeat with your right arm. Do this 10 times.

© Carson Dellosa Education

Fractions/Parts of Speech

Add or subtract. Write answers in simplest form.

1. $\dfrac{3}{4} + \dfrac{3}{8} =$ _____

2. $\dfrac{2}{7} + \dfrac{5}{6} =$ _____

3. $2\dfrac{1}{2} + \dfrac{2}{7} =$ _____

4. $2\dfrac{1}{3} - \dfrac{5}{12} =$ _____

5. $4\dfrac{7}{12} - \dfrac{3}{4} =$ _____

6. $5\dfrac{1}{4} - 1\dfrac{7}{8} =$ _____

Write >, <, or = to compare each pair of fractions.

7. $\dfrac{7}{15}$ ◯ $\dfrac{9}{15}$

8. $\dfrac{3}{4}$ ◯ $\dfrac{6}{8}$

9. $\dfrac{4}{6}$ ◯ $\dfrac{1}{3}$

10. $\dfrac{5}{9}$ ◯ $\dfrac{5}{8}$

11. $\dfrac{7}{8}$ ◯ $\dfrac{14}{16}$

12. $\dfrac{9}{9}$ ◯ $\dfrac{8}{8}$

Underline the complete perfect-tense verb in each sentence.

13. George had explained the plot of the movie to his brother.

14. Oliver had tried all the flavors of yogurt made by Yummy-Yo.

15. Zara has visited her grandma in Toronto twice this year.

16. By Thursday, the Desmonds will have returned from vacation.

17. Alice has been excited about the school dance all day.

18. Rachel will have played piano for six years this June.

19. Roberto had hoped the storm would pass before the game.

20. I will have read all the books on the top shelf by the end of the month.

Ancient Greece

Read the passage. Then, answer the questions.

The people of Ancient Greece lived nearly 4,000 years ago. They created beautiful buildings, and they held the first Olympic Games. The original Olympics were held every four years for more than 1,000 years. The Greeks also came up with the idea of democracy, or government by the people rather than government by a single ruler. The Greeks created small figurines and life-sized statues. They built public buildings, like theaters and stadiums. Modern sports arenas are still based on ancient Greek stadiums.

The Ancient Greeks made many contributions to medicine, trading, and literature. Greek medical texts were used for hundreds of years. Because Greece is made up of several islands, many Greeks were fishermen and sailors. They established trade routes throughout the ancient world. The Greek poet Homer wrote two epic poems that are still read today. The *Iliad* and *The Odyssey* told the stories of heroes who traveled the world.

21. What is the main idea of this passage?

    A. The ancient Greeks had many accomplishments in art, math, sports, and more.

    B. The ancient Greeks lived nearly 4,000 years ago.

    C. The ancient Greeks held the first Olympic Games.

22. Name three accomplishments of the ancient Greeks. _____

_____

23. What is one way that Greek architecture influenced modern buildings?

_____

24. How does the author support the topic sentence in paragraph 2? _____

_____

25. How can you tell that the Greeks' accomplishments in medicine were admired?

_____

Fractions/Punctuation

DAY 20

Write each equivalent fraction.

1. $\frac{3}{4} = \frac{}{8}$
2. $\frac{5}{8} = \frac{}{16}$
3. $\frac{10}{25} = \frac{2}{}$
4. $\frac{4}{9} = \frac{}{36}$

5. $\frac{7}{12} = \frac{28}{}$
6. $\frac{6}{6} = \frac{12}{}$
7. $\frac{3}{4} = \frac{}{20}$
8. $\frac{7}{15} = \frac{}{45}$

9. $\frac{9}{12} = \frac{36}{}$
10. $\frac{2}{3} = \frac{10}{}$
11. $\frac{3}{10} = \frac{18}{}$
12. $\frac{1}{3} = \frac{3}{}$

Each sentence is missing a comma. Use this proofreading mark to add each comma needed: ⁁

13. Meanwhile Mom and Dad wrapped Diego's gifts.

14. After the storm had blown over Grandpa went outside to survey the damage.

15. You haven't locked your keys in the car have you?

16. Yes I think the outfit you're wearing is appropriate for the recital.

17. Furthermore you didn't do any of your chores this week.

18. Did you remember to lock the back door Danny?

19. Next mix the milk, oil, and egg into the dry ingredients.

20. Dr. Alonzo have you received the results of the tests yet?

Vocabulary/Numbers

Read each pair of sentences. Circle the word in the first sentence that is the antonym for the bold word in the second sentence.

21. Ben enjoys Saturdays because he goes to his grandparents' farm.

    He **dislikes** when it is time to leave them and their farm animals.

22. Hurricanes and tornadoes can destroy anything in their paths.

    Sometimes, it takes months to **repair** the damage they cause.

23. When Nancy is at the park, she often plays on the swings.

    She **seldom** has to wait to take her turn.

24. It was foolish of Ricky not to study for the science test.

    When he saw his grade, he wished that he had been more **sensible** and had studied for it.

Round each number to the nearest tenth.

25. 5.684 _____

26. 0.374 _____

27. 2.415 _____

28. 3.012 _____

29. 8.542 _____

30. 0.894 _____

Round each number to the nearest hundredth.

31. 2.154 _____

32. 0.947 _____

33. 3.249 _____

34. 9.893 _____

35. 7.109 _____

36. 5.005 _____

Fast Fun Fact

Canada has more lakes than the rest of the world combined.

Science Experiment

Growing Crystals

Have you ever looked closely at ice crystals? What about salt crystals? In this activity, you can grow all kinds of crystals yourself!

Materials
- 10 tsp. water
- 1 tsp. ammonia
- pie pan
- 5 tsp. salt
- food coloring
- teaspoon
- 5 tsp. laundry bluing
- charcoal briquettes
- bowl

Procedure

1. With an adult, mix the water, salt, laundry bluing, and ammonia in a bowl.
2. Place the charcoal pieces in the pie pan. Pour just enough of the solution over the charcoal so that it covers the bottom of the pan.
3. To make colorful crystals, drizzle the food coloring over the top of the pile of charcoal. Or, to make white crystals with a blue tint, do not use any food coloring.
4. Crystals will begin to form right away on the charcoal and in the pan. As the solution evaporates, add more to the pan. Caution: If you pour the solution directly on the charcoal, the crystals, which are very fragile, will be crushed. Even blowing hard on the crystals will knock them over.

What's This All About?
Charcoal is a porous material. It absorbs the liquid in the bottom of the pie pan, and the liquid that is poured over it evaporates, leaving a crystal garden. The garden will continue to grow until the pan runs out of the solution or until the crystals grow too tall to support their own weight and fall.

Take a picture of the results of your experiment. Write a letter or an e-mail to a friend or family member and include the photo. Explain the steps of the experiment, as well as the process that occurred to create the crystals.

Air Pressure

How does the carbon dioxide in Earth's atmosphere affect the air temperature?

Materials

- 2 aquarium thermometers
- 2 clear plastic storage containers with lids
- 2 identical lamps with 200-watt bulbs
- 2 effervescent antacid and pain reliever tablets
- water
- tape
- ruler

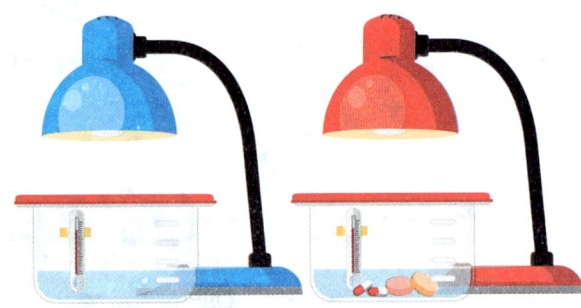

Procedure

1. Place the aquarium thermometers approximately 1 inch (2.5 cm) below the opening of the plastic storage containers so that they can be read from the outside. Tape the thermometers in place.
2. Add water to each plastic storage container to a depth of approximately 1.5 inches (3.8 cm). Place the lid on each container.
3. Lift the lid on one container slightly and quickly drop in two effervescent antacid and pain reliever tablets. The tablets will react with the water to produce carbon dioxide gas. Close the lid quickly to trap the carbon dioxide gas within the "atmosphere" of the container. Label the container.
4. Place one lamp above each container. The distance and location of the lamp above each container should be identical.
5. Take a temperature reading every 10 minutes until three consecutive readings are the same for each container. Record your readings in a graph.

What's This All About?

Burning fossil fuels to obtain energy creates chemical by-products that are dangerous in the atmosphere. Carbon dioxide, a greenhouse gas, is one chemical by-product that concerns many scientists. They think that the increase of carbon dioxide in the atmosphere is affecting the planet's temperatures. The carbon dioxide in the atmosphere absorbs solar energy and traps excess heat. Within this century, carbon dioxide levels have risen, as have global temperatures.

Social Studies Activity

The 50 States

Label as many U.S. states as you can. Use an atlas to finish if you need help.

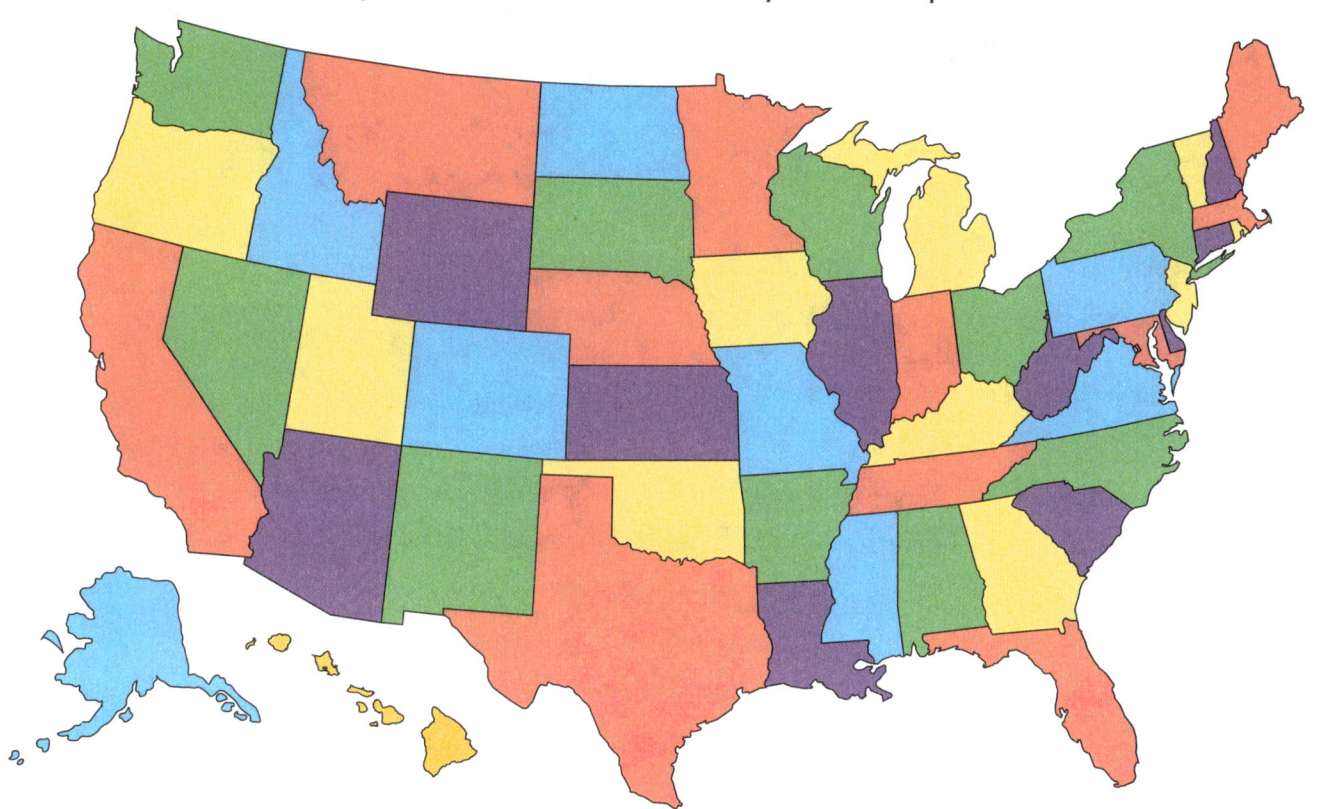

Alabama (AL)	Alaska (AK)	Arizona (AZ)	Arkansas (AR)
California (CA)	Colorado (CO)	Connecticut (CT)	Delaware (DE)
Florida (FL)	Georgia (GA)	Hawaii (HI)	Idaho (ID)
Illinois (IL)	Indiana (IN)	Iowa (IA)	Kansas (KS)
Kentucky (KY)	Louisiana (LA)	Maine (ME)	Maryland (MD)
Massachusetts (MA)	Michigan (MI)	Minnesota (MN)	Mississippi (MS)
Missouri (MO)	Montana (MT)	Nebraska (NE)	Nevada (NV)
New Hampshire (NH)	New Jersey (NJ)	New Mexico (NM)	New York (NY)
North Carolina (NC)	North Dakota (ND)	Ohio (OH)	Oklahoma (OK)
Oregon (OR)	Pennsylvania (PA)	Rhode Island (RI)	South Carolina (SC)
South Dakota (SD)	Tennessee (TN)	Texas (TX)	Utah (UT)
Vermont (VT)	Virginia (VA)	Washington (WA)	West Virginia (WV)
Wisconsin (WI)	Wyoming (WY)		

Social Studies Activity

U.S. States and Capitals

Match each U.S. state with its capital city.

a. Montpelier	n. Salem	A. Salt Lake City	N. Helena
b. Honolulu	o. Boston	B. Lansing	O. Cheyenne
c. Hartford	p. Pierre	C. Bismarck	P. Topeka
d. Lincoln	q. Sacramento	D. Annapolis	Q. Richmond
e. Columbus	r. Frankfort	E. Nashville	R. Trenton
f. Madison	s. Montgomery	F. Juneau	S. Boise
g. St. Paul	t. Augusta	G. Harrisburg	T. Albany
h. Springfield	u. Raleigh	H. Dover	U. Jackson
i. Phoenix	v. Austin	I. Carson City	V. Columbia
j. Des Moines	w. Concord	J. Little Rock	W. Baton Rouge
k. Providence	x. Tallahassee	K. Indianapolis	X. Atlanta
l. Olympia	y. Jefferson City	L. Denver	Y. Charleston
m. Santa Fe		M. Oklahoma City	

1. _____ Alabama
2. _____ Alaska
3. _____ Arizona
4. _____ Arkansas
5. _____ California
6. _____ Colorado
7. _____ Connecticut
8. _____ Delaware
9. _____ Florida
10. _____ Georgia
11. _____ Hawaii
12. _____ Idaho
13. _____ Illinois
14. _____ Indiana
15. _____ Iowa
16. _____ Kansas
17. _____ Kentucky
18. _____ Louisiana
19. _____ Maine
20. _____ Maryland
21. _____ Massachusetts
22. _____ Michigan
23. _____ Minnesota
24. _____ Mississippi
25. _____ Missouri
26. _____ Montana
27. _____ Nebraska
28. _____ Nevada
29. _____ New Hampshire
30. _____ New Jersey
31. _____ New Mexico
32. _____ New York
33. _____ North Carolina
34. _____ North Dakota
35. _____ Ohio
36. _____ Oklahoma
37. _____ Oregon
38. _____ Pennsylvania
39. _____ Rhode Island
40. _____ South Carolina
41. _____ South Dakota
42. _____ Tennessee
43. _____ Texas
44. _____ Utah
45. _____ Vermont
46. _____ Virginia
47. _____ Washington
48. _____ West Virginia
49. _____ Wisconsin
50. _____ Wyoming

Social Studies Activity

The 50 States

Label as many U.S. states as you can. Use an atlas to finish if you need help.

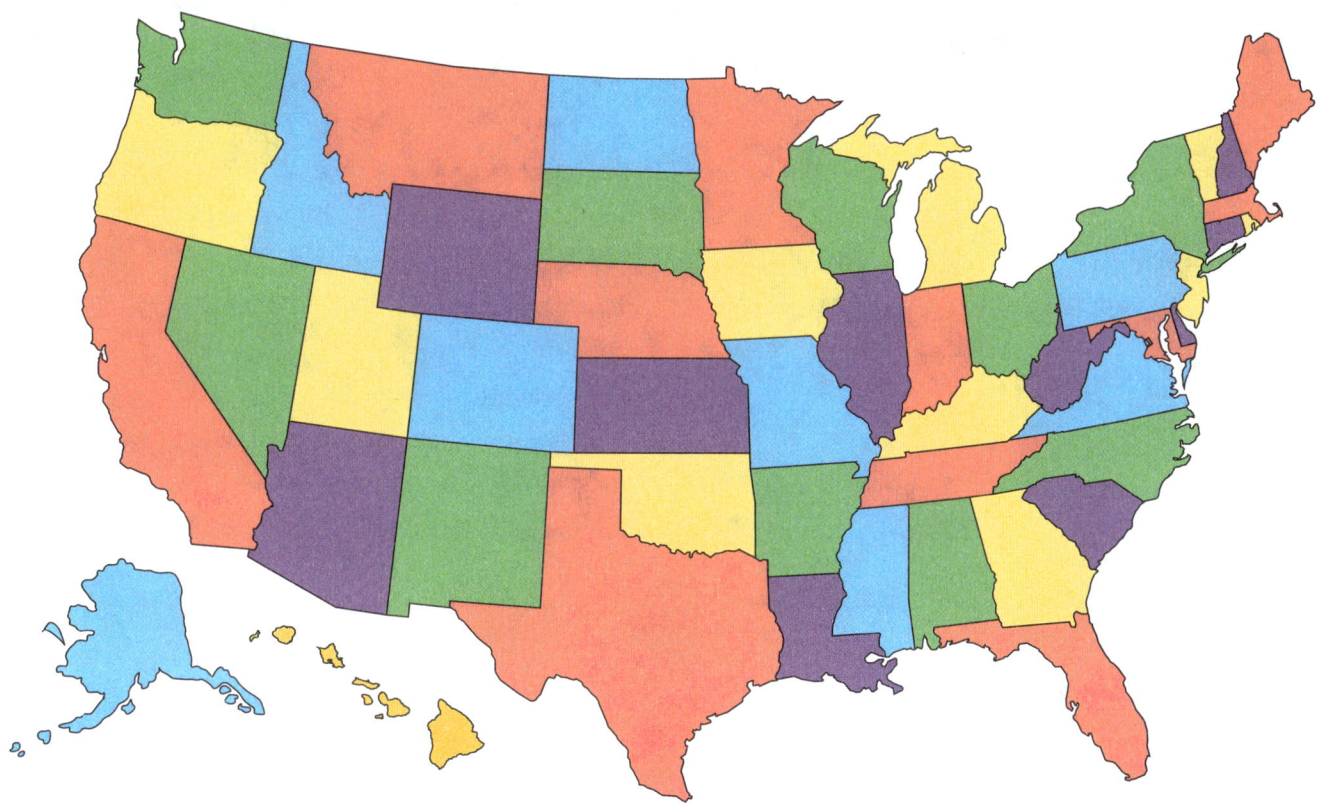

Alabama (AL)	Alaska (AK)	Arizona (AZ)	Arkansas (AR)
California (CA)	Colorado (CO)	Connecticut (CT)	Delaware (DE)
Florida (FL)	Georgia (GA)	Hawaii (HI)	Idaho (ID)
Illinois (IL)	Indiana (IN)	Iowa (IA)	Kansas (KS)
Kentucky (KY)	Louisiana (LA)	Maine (ME)	Maryland (MD)
Massachusetts (MA)	Michigan (MI)	Minnesota (MN)	Mississippi (MS)
Missouri (MO)	Montana (MT)	Nebraska (NE)	Nevada (NV)
New Hampshire (NH)	New Jersey (NJ)	New Mexico (NM)	New York (NY)
North Carolina (NC)	North Dakota (ND)	Ohio (OH)	Oklahoma (OK)
Oregon (OR)	Pennsylvania (PA)	Rhode Island (RI)	South Carolina (SC)
South Dakota (SD)	Tennessee (TN)	Texas (TX)	Utah (UT)
Vermont (VT)	Virginia (VA)	Washington (WA)	West Virginia (WV)
Wisconsin (WI)	Wyoming (WY)		

U.S. States and Capitals

Match each U.S. state with its capital city.

a. Montpelier	n. Salem	A. Salt Lake City	N. Helena
b. Honolulu	o. Boston	B. Lansing	O. Cheyenne
c. Hartford	p. Pierre	C. Bismarck	P. Topeka
d. Lincoln	q. Sacramento	D. Annapolis	Q. Richmond
e. Columbus	r. Frankfort	E. Nashville	R. Trenton
f. Madison	s. Montgomery	F. Juneau	S. Boise
g. St. Paul	t. Augusta	G. Harrisburg	T. Albany
h. Springfield	u. Raleigh	H. Dover	U. Jackson
i. Phoenix	v. Austin	I. Carson City	V. Columbia
j. Des Moines	w. Concord	J. Little Rock	W. Baton Rouge
k. Providence	x. Tallahassee	K. Indianapolis	X. Atlanta
l. Olympia	y. Jefferson City	L. Denver	Y. Charleston
m. Santa Fe		M. Oklahoma City	

1. _____ Alabama
2. _____ Alaska
3. _____ Arizona
4. _____ Arkansas
5. _____ California
6. _____ Colorado
7. _____ Connecticut
8. _____ Delaware
9. _____ Florida
10. _____ Georgia
11. _____ Hawaii
12. _____ Idaho
13. _____ Illinois
14. _____ Indiana
15. _____ Iowa
16. _____ Kansas
17. _____ Kentucky
18. _____ Louisiana
19. _____ Maine
20. _____ Maryland
21. _____ Massachusetts
22. _____ Michigan
23. _____ Minnesota
24. _____ Mississippi
25. _____ Missouri
26. _____ Montana
27. _____ Nebraska
28. _____ Nevada
29. _____ New Hampshire
30. _____ New Jersey
31. _____ New Mexico
32. _____ New York
33. _____ North Carolina
34. _____ North Dakota
35. _____ Ohio
36. _____ Oklahoma
37. _____ Oregon
38. _____ Pennsylvania
39. _____ Rhode Island
40. _____ South Carolina
41. _____ South Dakota
42. _____ Tennessee
43. _____ Texas
44. _____ Utah
45. _____ Vermont
46. _____ Virginia
47. _____ Washington
48. _____ West Virginia
49. _____ Wisconsin
50. _____ Wyoming

Social Studies Activity

Where I Live

Draw the shape of your state or province and label where you live. Draw your state or province's flower and bird.

SECTION 2

Monthly Goals

Think of three goals to set for yourself this month. For example, you may want to read for 30 minutes each day. Write your goals on the lines. Post them someplace where you will see them every day.

Draw a line through each goal as you meet it. Feel proud that you have met your goals and set new ones to continue to challenge yourself.

1. _____
2. _____
3. _____

Word List

The following words are used in this section. Use a dictionary to look up each word that you do not know. Write three sentences. Use a word from the word list in each sentence.

align
archaeologists
elaborate
epicenter
manor

raid
shortcut
tiers
untidy
wombat

1. _____
_____
2. _____
_____
3. _____
_____

Introduction to Strength

This section includes Let's Play Today and Mindful Moments activities that focus on strength. These activities are designed to help you spend less time on a screen and more time developing healthy emotional and physical habits. If you have limited mobility, feel free to modify any suggested activity or choose a different one from the list on the following page.

Like flexibility, strength is necessary to be healthy. You might think being strong means lifting an enormous amount of weight. But strength is much more than just the ability to pick up heavy barbells. Strength is built by being physically active on a daily basis. When you were younger, you walked and ran slower. Now all of your movements are much faster. Look how strong you've become!

Everyday activities, fun exercises, and enjoyable games help you gain strength. Take a walk, do exercises like push-ups or squats, or play a game of basketball or tag to build your physical strength.

Set realistic, achievable goals to improve your physical strength based on your ability and the activities you enjoy. Over the summer months, keep track of these goals and celebrate when you achieve them. Then set new ones!

Having strength of character on the inside is just as important as having physical strength on the outside. Being a strong person on the inside can be shown by being honest, facing a fear, helping others, standing up for someone who needs a friend, or choosing to do the right thing when presented with a difficult situation. Think about times when you have had inner strength that has helped you handle a situation.

Engaging Online Practice

Bring learning to life with fun, interactive activities on IXL! Look for the Skill ID box and type the 3-digit code into the search bar on IXL.com or the IXL mobile app. Ten questions per day are free!

Skill IDs
5UN • D9K

© Carson Dellosa Education

SECTION 2

Let's Play Today

Get up and moving with these Let's Play Today activities. Section 2 focuses on strength. Strengthening exercises make your bones and muscles stronger. Strong bones and muscles help prevent injury and speed up recovery from injury. Use this list in addition to or as a replacement for any Let's Play Today suggestions on the activity pages. This list was developed to be inclusive of a variety of abilities. Choose the ones that are a good fit for you! Make modifications as needed. These activities may require adult supervision. See page 2 for full caution information.

Lava Pit:
Hop from pillow to pillow on an imaginary bed of lava. Start with just 3-4 pillows and repeat it two times. Over time, gradually add pillows to work up to a longer, more complex path of pillows. Repeat hopping on the longer path 10 times.

Frog Hops:
Crouch down with your hands on the floor in a frog-like position. Hop forward like a frog 3-4 times. Over time, gradually increase the number of hops until you get to 15.

Shadow Fun:
Go outside on a sunny day and stand so you can see your shadow. If you are by yourself, practice shadow boxing. Bend your arms at the elbows and bring your hands back to your body. Make a fist with each hand. Extend one arm at a time to mimic a boxing motion. If someone is outside with you, trace each other's shadow with sidewalk chalk. Hold a pose that works your muscles, such as standing on one leg or flexing your arms.

Balloon Back-and-Forth:
Either seated or standing, hit a balloon up into the air to another person. That person will hit it back to you. Keep track of how many times you can hit it to each other without it touching the ground. Try to increase your score.

Swim Like a Fish:
Wearing a life jacket in the shallow end of a pool, try swimming like a fish. Use flippers to help. See how many different ways to swim you can come up with. For example, swim like you have a fish tail, swim without using your arms, swim with flippers on your hands, or roll around.

© Carson Dellosa Education

Fractions/Punctuation

DAY 1

Change each fraction into an equivalent mixed number.

1. $\frac{56}{6}$ = _____
2. $\frac{14}{4}$ = _____
3. $\frac{38}{8}$ = _____
4. $\frac{52}{8}$ = _____

5. $\frac{18}{4}$ = _____
6. $\frac{35}{5}$ = _____
7. $\frac{14}{6}$ = _____
8. $\frac{10}{8}$ = _____

Find the fraction of each number.

9. $\frac{2}{5}$ of 10 = _____
10. $\frac{1}{4}$ of 32 = _____

11. $\frac{4}{6}$ of 24 = _____
12. $\frac{3}{5}$ of 60 = _____

Are the commas in each sentence used correctly? Write *yes* or *no*.

13. The students visited Philadelphia, Pennsylvania and New, York. _____

14. They saw museums, of art, history and science in Philadelphia. _____

15. Don, Debbie, and Yusef toured Independence Hall. _____

Add commas where they are needed in each sentence.

16. Debbie Don and Yusef were impressed with New York City.

17. The Bronx Manhattan Queens Brooklyn and Staten Island are its five boroughs.

18. Chinatown Greenwich Village and Harlem are three neighborhoods in Manhattan.

Mindful Moment

Think of a person you admire. Draw a picture of this person and write a paragraph about why you admire them. Then give it to them!

DAY 1 — Vocabulary/Reading Comprehension

Write a synonym for each word.

19. jump _____

20. quickly _____

21. tired _____

22. sprint _____

Write an antonym for each word.

23. narrow _____

24. near _____

25. horrible _____

26. open _____

Read the paragraph. Then, answer the questions.

    Earth is like a huge magnet. It has a magnetic field. Its magnetism is the strongest at the north and south poles. When a rock forms, magnetic particles within the rock align themselves with Earth's magnetic field. They will point toward either the north or south pole. There are some rocks that do not point to the current north and south poles. Scientists conclude that either the north and south poles have moved, or the rocks themselves have moved since they first formed. Most scientists think that the rocks and continents have moved. Geologists use this information to determine how the continents have moved over time.

27. Why is Earth compared to a magnet? _____

28. Where are Earth's strongest points of magnetism? _____

29. How can geologists study the movements of the continents? _____

_____

Fractions/Vocabulary

To multiply fractions, first multiply the numerators. Then, multiply the denominators. When you multiply two fractions, the product is smaller than the two factors. Find each product. Simplify each fraction. Then, draw a fraction picture to illustrate each answer.

1. $\frac{1}{2} \times \frac{3}{4} =$ _____

2. $\frac{1}{4} \times \frac{1}{2} =$ _____

3. $\frac{1}{3} \times \frac{2}{3} =$ _____

4. $\frac{2}{3} \times \frac{4}{5} =$ _____

5. $\frac{2}{3} \times \frac{2}{3} =$ _____

6. $\frac{3}{4} \times \frac{2}{5} =$ _____

Complete each sentence with a word from the word bank. Capitalize a word if needed.

| however | nevertheless | moreover |
| although | similarly | in addition |

7. Mr. Oh was supposed to pick up Susan at 4:00. _____, the heavy traffic caused him to be 15 minutes late.

8. _____ it hasn't rained in almost two weeks, our vegetable garden is doing well.

9. Gabriela has six chickens _____ to a dog, a rabbit, three cats, and a goldfish.

10. The weather for our picnic was a bit soggy, but the day was fun _____.

11. To Kill a Mockingbird is a classic American novel. _____, it's a very moving story.

12. A female kangaroo carries her baby in her pouch for about nine months. _____, a mother wombat carries her baby in her pouch for the first half year of its life.

Reading Comprehension

Read the passage. Then, answer the questions.

The Mayan Empire

The Maya lived in Central America from about 2600 BCE to about 900 CE. The Mayan Empire covered present-day Guatemala, Belize, and El Salvador, as well as part of Honduras and southeastern Mexico. The Maya built elaborate stone temples, palaces, and buildings called *observatories* from which they could watch the movements of the planets and stars. They created a calendar with 260 days to mark special days in their civilization. Every 20th day, the Maya held a festival.

The Mayan ruins in Chichén Itzá, Mexico, include performance stages, markets, and even a ball court. Many Mayan foods are still eaten in Central America, including maize (corn), beans, chili peppers, and squash. The Maya wore beautiful woven fabrics, feathered headdresses, and hats. No one is sure why the Maya disappeared, but archaeologists hope to find out.

13. What is the main idea of this passage?

    A. The Maya built many great buildings.

    B. The Maya suddenly disappeared.

    C. The Maya lived in Central America thousands of years ago.

14. What are the approximate dates when the Maya lived in Central America? _____
_____

15. Which modern countries did the Mayan Empire cover? _____
_____

16. What was special about the Mayan calendar? _____
_____
_____

17. Reread the last sentence of the passage. What purpose does it serve? Is it an effective ending for the passage? Why or why not? _____
_____
_____

Fractions/Parts of Speech

DAY 3

Find each product. Simplify each fraction.

1. $\frac{1}{2} \times \frac{3}{5} = $ _____

2. $\frac{2}{3} \times \frac{2}{3} = $ _____

3. $\frac{4}{5} \times \frac{2}{7} = $ _____

4. $\frac{1}{2} \times \frac{1}{6} \times \frac{2}{3} = $ _____

5. $\frac{2}{3} \times \frac{5}{6} \times \frac{1}{4} = $ _____

6. $\frac{1}{3} \times \frac{5}{7} \times \frac{3}{5} = $ _____

Replace each underlined word with a preposition from the word bank to show a different relationship between the words in each sentence.

| behind | near | through | under | until |

7. Grayson found his backpack ~~under~~ _____near_____ his desk.

8. Julie stood <u>beside</u> _____ me at the parade.

9. Did you leave this box <u>on</u> _____ the bench?

10. The children will play <u>after</u> _____ dark.

11. The bats flew <u>into</u> _____ the window.

The object of the preposition is the noun or pronoun following a preposition. Write an object (noun or pronoun) for each underlined preposition.

12. That child had a glass <u>of</u> _____ .

13. We climbed <u>over</u> a _____ .

14. Jayla fell <u>off</u> her _____ .

15. Far <u>below</u> the _____ , we could see the river.

DAY 3

Vocabulary/Social Studies

Skill IDs: 7ZU • 2KY — Search for these skill IDs on IXL.com for more practice!

Write the homophone in parentheses that matches each definition. Use a dictionary if you need help.

16. _____ : grinds or crushes with the teeth (chews, choose)

17. _____ : inexpensive; of little value (cheap, cheep)

18. _____ : a large mammal with shaggy fur (bare, bear)

19. _____ : having little or no color; not bright (pail, pale)

20. _____ : a house on a large estate (manner, manor)

21. _____ : a series of rows, one above another (tears, tiers)

Use the time line to answer each question about the events leading up to the Revolutionary War.

1754	1763	1765	1770	1773	1774	1775
French and Indian War	King George III limits Western settlement	Stamp Act	Boston Massacre	Boston Tea Party	Intolerable Acts	Battles fought at Lexington and Concord

22. How many years after the French and Indian War did the Boston Massacre occur?
_____

23. Which events occurred in Boston? Circle them on the time line.

24. Which occurred first—the Stamp Act or the Intolerable Acts? How many years were between these events? _____

25. Who gave a proclamation to limit Western settlement? _____

26. Where were the battles fought in 1775? _____

Let's Play Today * See page 60.

With feet shoulder-width apart, do a squat pose by leaning back like you're sitting in a chair. Then stand back up. See how many squats you can do in 30 seconds.

Fractions/Parts of Speech

DAY 4

Match each term with its definition.

1. _____ fraction
2. _____ fraction greater than 1
3. _____ quotient
4. _____ mixed number
5. _____ denominator
6. _____ numerator

A. the answer you get when you divide one number by another number

B. the number found below the line in a fraction

C. a number that names a part of a set or whole

D. the number found above the line in a fraction

E. a number that has a whole number and a fraction

F. a fraction whose numerator is greater than or equal to its denominator

Fill in each blank.

7. Write 2 ÷ 9 as a fraction. _____

8. Write 15 ÷ 7 as a fraction greater than 1. _____

9. What kind of fractions are $\frac{28}{5}$ and $\frac{59}{7}$? _____

   Write a mixed number for each fraction. _____

A prepositional phrase is made up of a preposition and its object. Circle each prepositional phrase.

10. between the bases   along the trail   until four o'clock

    near the window   the circus elephant   the math problem

    a hanging light   outside the door   are the bridges

    the wet streets   under the house   in the barn

    things that have gills your guide   how you will be

Language Arts

Circle the correct homophone(s) to complete each sentence.

11. Tanya (new, **knew**) how to get along with (**new**, knew) people.

12. The (our, **hour**) hand on (**our**, hour) new clock does not move correctly.

13. I like to (**read**, reed) magazines about sports.

14. You can (**buy**, by) a good used TV in the store next (**to**, two, too) the shopping mall.

15. Spencer and Jack invited me to come to (there, **their**) house after school.

16. The students had to bring (to, **two**, too) pencils to class for the test.

17. I (**see**, sea) a beautiful sunset down by the (see, **sea**) every night.

18. Our cat, Cosby, sometimes chases its (tale, **tail**).

Idioms are phrases that aren't meant to be taken literally. Match the idiom in bold on the left with its meaning on the right.

19. _____ Lana and I are good friends, but she **gave me the cold shoulder** at school.

    A. aware of everything going on around them

20. _____ My dad's joke **cracked us up**!

    B. to treat someone in an unfriendly way

21. _____ My teacher has **eyes in the back of her head**, so we don't misbehave in class.

    C. having to start all over

22. _____ Juan **cut corners** on his project because he was in a hurry.

    D. made us laugh

23. _____ My teacher said I did the math problem all wrong, so it was **back to square one**.

    E. to take a shortcut when working

© Carson Dellosa Education

Fractions/Grammar

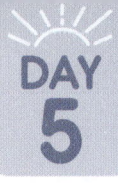

Skill IDs: DS2 • RMV

DAY 5

To divide fractions, multiply the first fraction by the reciprocal of the second fraction. Then simplify the quotient if needed.

1. $\dfrac{2}{3} \div \dfrac{4}{5} = \dfrac{2}{3} \times \dfrac{5}{4} = \dfrac{10}{12} = \dfrac{5}{6}$

2. $\dfrac{3}{4} \div \dfrac{1}{2} =$

3. $\dfrac{1}{5} \div \dfrac{3}{10} =$

4. $\dfrac{1}{6} \div \dfrac{1}{12} =$

5. $\dfrac{4}{5} \div \dfrac{2}{3} =$

6. $\dfrac{2}{8} \div \dfrac{3}{4} =$

7. $\dfrac{6}{7} \div \dfrac{8}{12} =$

8. $\dfrac{1}{5} \div \dfrac{1}{2} =$

9. $\dfrac{9}{12} \div \dfrac{8}{10} =$

Write *and*, *or*, or *but* to complete each sentence.

10. Jenna _____ LaTeisha are on the same softball team.

11. Jenna wanted the team color to be blue, _____ LaTeisha preferred red.

12. The players chose their favorite positions, _____ they were very pleased.

13. Jenna plays either first base _____ in the outfield.

14. In the first inning, Jenna hit a single, _____ LaTeisha hit a double.

15. Their team was winning, _____ the other team caught up in the fourth inning.

Fast Fun Fact

Jupiter is so large that more than 1,300 Earths could fit inside of it!

Read the passage. Then, answer the questions.

Harriet Tubman

Harriet Tubman used the Underground Railroad, a secret system of safe houses and people, to escape from slavery. Tubman went to Philadelphia, Pennsylvania, where she could live as a free person. Escaping from slavery was hard and dangerous. But Tubman was brave, and once she was free, she wanted to help others become free too. She returned to the South and helped her family members and other enslaved people escape. Harriet Tubman worked on the Underground Railroad from 1850 to 1860.

When the Civil War started, Tubman became a spy. Many women worked as spies during the war, but few took as many risks as Tubman did. Tubman knew the land in the South, and she knew ways to travel without being caught. She gathered information to help the Northern army. Tubman even led a group of Black soldiers on a raid. The group freed more than 700 enslaved people. No woman had led American soldiers on a raid before. Tubman also worked as a nurse. She cared for wounded Black soldiers and enslaved people. After the war, Tubman helped the freed people. She opened her home to take care of the elderly, and she worked for women's rights. Harriet Tubman was one of the strongest and bravest women in American history.

16. What is the main idea of this passage?

    A. Harriet Tubman was a strong woman.

    B. Harriet Tubman was an enslaved person who escaped.

    C. Harriet Tubman was a strong woman who spent her life helping others.

17. Number the events in the order they happened.

    _____ Tubman worked for women's rights.

    _____ Tubman escaped to freedom in the North.

    _____ Tubman worked as a spy.

    _____ Tubman's work helping enslaved people escape ended when the war started.

18. What did Tubman do during the war that no other woman had ever done?

    _____

19. Name something Tubman did after the war. _____

20. Describe the author's point of view. How do they feel about Harriet Tubman? How do you know? _____

    _____

Decimals/Parts of Speech

When adding or subtracting decimals, first line up the decimals. If the amount of decimal places in the numbers is not the same, add zeros to the end of the number with fewer decimal places. Solve each problem.

1. 3.45 + 5.923 =

    $$\begin{array}{r}\overset{1}{3.450}\\+5.923\\\hline 9.373\end{array}$$

2. 34.09 - 9.407 =

3. 3.806 + 5.29 =

4. 185.04 - 165.9 =

5. 42.881 + 8.96 =

6. $224.00 - $116.98 =

Write an interjection from the word bank on each line. Use an exclamation point to show strong emotion. Use a comma to show weaker emotion.

| Great | Hey | Oh | Oh no | Phew | Wow | Yes |

7. _____ why is the classroom so busy today?

8. _____ I forgot that we are pretending to build a pyramid.

9. _____ It looks like ancient Egypt!

10. _____ We tried to decorate in an ancient style.

11. _____ Millie remembered to wear her costume.

12. _____ I almost forgot to bring mine!

13. _____ I remembered that it was in my backpack!

Numbers/Writing

Multiply or divide by powers of ten. In your answer, is the number of zeros correct? Did you place the decimal point correctly?

14. $19 \times 10^5 = $ _____

15. $.652 \div 10^3 = $ _____

16. $.54 \times 10^8 = $ _____

17. $201 \times 10^2 = $ _____

18. $80{,}000 \times 10^3 = $ _____

19. $.714 \times 10^4 = $ _____

20. $.2 \div 10^6 = $ _____

21. $.857 \times 10^1 = $ _____

22. $75 \times 10^9 = $ _____

23. $1.52 \times 10^4 = $ _____

24. $50 \times 10^5 = $ _____

25. $235.48 \div 10^2 = $ _____

You have just learned that you will share a bedroom with a younger brother or sister. Write a paragraph explaining why you feel that this is or is not a good idea.

_____
_____
_____
_____
_____
_____
_____
_____

Mindful Moment

Lying on the floor with a stuffed animal on your chest, slowly take in a deep breath. Then slowly let it out. Watch the animal rise and fall with each deep breath.

Data Analysis/Spelling

Fill in the table with information from the passage.

Astrid opened a checking account on May 15 with $500.25. On May 31, she deposited $496.80. On June 4, she withdrew $145.00 to buy some clothes. On June 15, she deposited $435.20. On June 30, she deposited $600.00. On July 1, she withdrew $463.00 to pay for camp. On July 15, she deposited $110.00. On July 24, she withdrew $600.00 to buy a computer.

Date	Deposit	Withdrawal	Total $
May 15	$500.25		$500.25
May 31			
June 4			
June 15			
June 30			
July 1			
July 15			
July 24			

Find the misspelled word in each group. Underline it and spell it correctly on the line.

1. joyous   genre   iceburg   _____

2. hatchet   symmetry   sieze   _____

3. commitee exterior   regret   _____

4. drowsy   oblige   demacratic   _____

5. mythical quotasion scenario   _____

6. destination slugish excel   _____

7. attire   opress   grievance   _____

8. plack   adopt   bankrupt   _____

Vocabulary/Writing

An analogy shows a relationship between two sets of words or phrases. Complete each analogy.

9. *Preview* is to *previewed* as *decide* is to __decided__.

10. *Hear* is to *ear* as *talk* is to _____.

11. *Griddle* is to *pancake* as *pot* is to _____.

12. *Author* is to *book* as *artist* is to _____.

13. *Business* is to *businesses* as *address* is to _____.

14. *Research* is to *researcher* as *garden* is to _____.

15. *Breakfast* is to *lunch* as *morning* is to _____.

16. *Control* is to *controllable* as *reason* is to _____.

17. *TV* is to *commercial* as *magazine* is to _____.

18. *Manager* is to *store* as *principal* is to _____.

Write step-by-step directions for something you know how to do well, such as taking care of a pet, creating a video, or playing an instrument. Use sequence words like *first*, *then*, *next*, and *last*.

_____
_____
_____
_____
_____
_____
_____
_____

Multiplication/Language Arts

DAY 8

Find each product. Add extra zeros when necessary.

1. 41.5 × 0.17
2. 1.09 × 0.68
3. 3.05 × 85.2
4. 0.003 × 3.9

5. 7.4 × 0.07
6. 0.09 × 2.3
7. 0.035 × 0.02
8. 0.005 × 55

On the line, write the type of figurative language that is in each sentence: *S* for simile, *M* for metaphor, *H* for hyperbole, or *P* for personification.

9. _____ The surface of the frozen lake glistened like glass as the sun set.

10. _____ At dawn, two small birds outside my window demanded that I get up immediately.

11. _____ I have asked you a million times to pick up your wet towels!

12. _____ The tornado was a train coming full speed at the town.

13. _____ Silas's hair was as shiny as a new copper penny.

14. _____ It's going to take me a hundred years to clean up this room.

15. _____ The sunflowers lifted their heavy heads and smiled at the late morning sun.

16. _____ Devon is a real tiger when he has his mind set on something.

Let's Play Today * See page 60.

Plank with a friend or family member and see who can hold their plank the longest.

Reading Comprehension

Read the poem. Then, answer the questions.

"Wild Geese" by Celia Thaxter

The wild wind blows, the sun shines, the birds sing loud,
The blue, blue sky is flecked with fleecy dappled cloud,
Over earth's rejoicing fields the children dance and sing,
And the frogs pipe in chorus, "It is spring! It is spring!"

The grass comes, the flower laughs where lately lay the snow,
O'er the breezy hill-top hoarsely calls the crow,
By the flowing river the alder catkins swing,
And the sweet song-sparrow cries, "Spring! It is spring!"

Hark, what a clamor goes winging through the sky!
Look, children! Listen to the sound so wild and high!
Like a **peal** of broken bells,—kling, klang, kling,—
Far and high the wild geese cry, "Spring! It is spring!"

Bear the winter off with you, O wild geese dear!
Carry all the cold away, far away from here;
Chase the snow into the north, O strong of heart and wing,
While we share the robin's rapture, crying "Spring! It is spring!"

17. Give one example of personification from the poem. _____
    _____

18. What does *peal* mean? _____
    _____

19. How does the poet feel about the coming of spring? Support your answer with details
    from the poem. _____
    _____
    _____
    _____
    _____

Multiplication/Vocabulary

Find each product.

1. 0.12
    × 6

2. 0.08
    × 7

3. 4.6
    × 3

4. 5.05
    × 8

5. 1.906
    × 28

6. 7.0216
    × 52

7. 6.65
    × 77

8. 27.035
    × 93

Complete each analogy.

9. *Tree* is to *lumber* as *wheat* is to ____flour____.

10. *Leg* is to *chair* as *shade* is to _____.

11. *Pages* are to *book* as _____ are to the *United States*.

12. *Finger* is to *hand* as *toe* is to _____.

13. *Brake* is to *stop* as *gas pedal* is to _____.

14. *Apple* is to *tree* as *grape* is to _____.

15. *Foal* is to *horse* as *puppy* is to _____.

16. *Space* is to *rocket* as _____ is to *car*.

17. *Bird* is to *nest* as *lion* is to _____.

18. *Playwright* is to *play* as *sculptor* is to _____.

DAY 9

Measurement

Find the volume of each rectangular solid by multiplying together the length, width, and height.

19.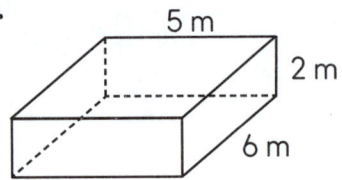

V = _____

20.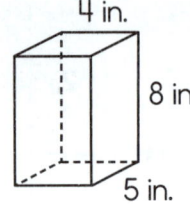

V = _____

21.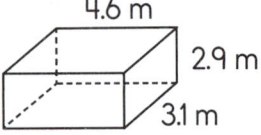

V = _____

22.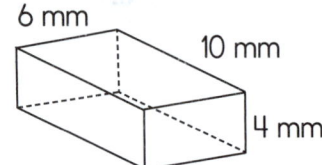

V = _____

23.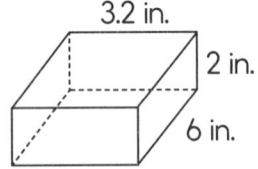

V = _____

24.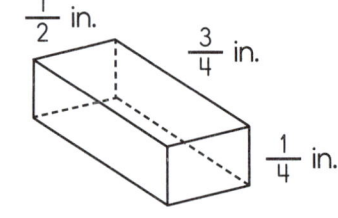

V = _____

Convert the given liquid measurements to new units.

1 gallon (gal.) = 4 quarts (qts.) = 8 pints (pts.) = 16 cups (C) = 128 fluid ounces (fl. oz.)

25. 8 qts. = _____ pts.

26. 4 gal. = _____ qts.

27. 16 fl. oz. = _____ pts.

28. 32 pts. = _____ qts.

29. 16 C = _____ qts.

30. 7 gal. = _____ C

Division/Grammar  Skill IDs 8FT • EXW

DAY 10

Find each quotient.

1. 3)5.4
2. 4)10.4
3. 7)25.9
4. 0.2)17.8

5. 3.4)80.24
6. 2.5)114.75
7. 1.9)149.15
8. 6.1)338.55

The noun that a pronoun refers to is called the pronoun's antecedent. A pronoun must agree with its antecedent. Underline the pronoun that best completes each sentence.

9. Micah and Azim stopped at the art room to pick up (their, his) paintings.

10. When Bella and Cameron arrived at the campground, (they, we) unloaded the car.

11. On Thursday, my mom and stepdad are going to the botanical gardens where (they, you) will see a new display of garden sculptures.

12. The coaches discussed (his, their) players in the teachers' lounge.

13. I asked the cashier at the grocery store, and (they, she) was very helpful.

14. Nicole and I planned (their, our) performance for weeks.

15. They like to visit parks where (they, it) can bring a dog.

16. When a person is kind to others, (you, he) will receive kindness in return.

 **Fast Fun Fact**
An ice-cream store in Delaware sells green ice cream called Booger!

Data Analysis/Science

Data can be described by how the values relate to each other and how they are spread out. Describe each set of data.

17. 4, 8, 9, 12, 12, 13, 14, 24, 27

   Lowest value: __4__   Highest value: __27__

   Spread: __23__   Center value: __12__

18. 44, 44, 45, 47, 48, 48, 49, 50, 52

   Lowest value: _____   Highest value: _____

   Spread: _____   Center value: _____

19. 10, 10, 25, 30, 45, 55, 80, 85, 95, 100, 100

   Lowest value: _____   Highest value: _____

   Spread: _____   Center value: _____

Write words from the word bank to complete the paragraph. With an adult, use the Internet for help.

| Seismologists | fault | earthquake | above | epicenter |
| Seismic waves | focus | energy | beneath | fracture |

An _____ is the sudden shaking of the ground that happens when _____ stored in rock is released. A _____ is a break, or _____, in Earth's crust. As rock breaks, stored energy moves along the fault. The hypocenter, or _____, is where an earthquake begins. The point on Earth's crust that is directly _____ the focus is called the _____. An earthquake begins _____ Earth's surface. _____, or shock waves, move out from the focus and cause the ground to shake. _____ study and record these shock waves and determine the size of the earthquake.

Add., Subt., Mult., & Div./Grammar

Solve each problem.

1.
```
   24.98
   14.20
   10.19
 + 82.29
```

2.
```
   86,945
    6,913
    7,428
 +  5,317
```

3.
```
     674
 ×   392
```

4.
```
   5,978
 ×   703
```

5. $72 \overline{)95{,}634}$

6. $82 \overline{)809{,}791}$

7. $6\frac{3}{5} \times 1\frac{2}{8} =$ _____

8. $2\frac{1}{2} + 6\frac{3}{4} =$ _____

9. $8 - 2\frac{3}{4} =$ _____

A sentence should clearly indicate the noun a pronoun refers to. Revise the underlined words to make the meaning of each sentence clear.

10. When the tree hit the telephone pole, <u>it burst into flames</u>.

    When the tree hit the telephone pole, the tree burst into flames.

11. When the president said good-bye to the senator, <u>she looked confident</u>. _____

12. Marty told Ben that his scrape would heal if <u>he put antiseptic on it</u>. _____

13. Before the key could fit the keyhole, <u>it had to be made smaller</u>. _____

14. Mateo told his dad that <u>his shirt</u> had a stain on it. _____

Search for this skill ID on IXL.com for more practice!

Reading Comprehension

Read the passage. Then, answer the questions.

from *The Story of Doctor Dolittle* by Hugh Lofting

He was very fond of animals and kept many kinds of pets. Besides the goldfish in the pond at the bottom of his garden, he had rabbits in the pantry, white mice in his piano, a squirrel in the linen closet and a hedgehog in the cellar. He had a cow with a calf too, and an old lame horse twenty-five years of age—and chickens, and pigeons, and two lambs, and many other animals. But his favorite pets were Dab-Dab the duck, Jip the dog, Gub-Gub the baby pig, Polynesia the parrot, and the owl Too-Too.

His sister used to grumble about all these animals and said they made the house untidy. And one day when an old lady with rheumatism came to see the Doctor, she sat on the hedgehog who was sleeping on the sofa and never came to see him any more, but drove every Saturday all the way to Oxenthorpe, another town ten miles off, to see a different doctor.

Then his sister, Sarah Dolittle, came to him and said, "John, how can you expect sick people to come and see you when you keep all these animals in the house? It's a fine doctor would have his parlor full of hedgehogs and mice!"

15. Based on the passage, what type of book do you think *The Story of Doctor Dolittle* is? Explain.

_____

_____

16. From what point of view is the story told? How might it be different if it were told from Dr. Dolittle's point of view? _____

_____

17. Watch the movie or listen to the audiobook of this story. Compare your experience reading the story with watching or listening to it. _____

_____

_____

_____

 **Mindful Moment**

What have you done lately that you are proud of? Finish this sentence: "I am proud of myself for/because . . ." Write a paragraph about it or tell a family member.

Multiplication & Division/Language Arts

Complete each fact family.

1. 78 × 42 = 3,276

   _____

   3,276 ÷ 42 = 78

   _____

2. 39 × 56 = 2,184

   _____

   _____

   _____

3. 151 × 27 = 4,077

   _____

   _____

   _____

4. 3,762 ÷ 38 = 99

   _____

   _____

   _____

5. 26,320 ÷ 47 = 560

   _____

   _____

   _____

6. 48,306 ÷ 83 = 582

   _____

   _____

   _____

A simile is a figure of speech in which two unlike things are compared using *like* or *as*. Write the actual meaning of each simile.

7. Her voice lilted like soft music. _____

8. The cat's fur is as smooth as silk. _____

9. The water is like a sparkling sapphire. _____

10. Kristen soaked up the information like a sponge. _____

11. He stood as straight as an arrow. _____

Write your own simile.

12. _____

DAY 12 — Algebra/Writing

IXL Skill ID **HMZ**

Write the missing part of each equation.

13. 67 × _____ = 603

14. _____ × 77 = 385

15. 2,210 ÷ _____ = 85

16. 5,518 ÷ _____ = 62

17. 19,347 - _____ = 18,470

18. 23,432 + _____ = 24,089

19. 32 × _____ = 6,400

20. 56,993 - _____ = 55,598

21. _____ + 34,561 = 40,090

22. 50,000 ÷ _____ = 1,250

23. 19,263 + _____ = 66,390

24. _____ - 80,399 = 110,099

You have been given the task of adding one month to the year. What would you call your month? When in the year would it occur? What would people celebrate during the month? Write a paragraph describing your new month.

_____

_____

_____

_____

_____

_____

Multiplication & Division/Grammar

A multiple is a number that may be divided by another number without leaving a remainder. List five multiples for each of the following numbers.

1. 2 ____4, 6, 8, 10, 12____
2. 5 _____
3. 9 _____
4. 12 _____

Common multiples are multiples that two or more numbers share. List three common multiples for each pair of numbers.

5. 4 and 5 ____20, 40, 60____
6. 3 and 4 _____
7. 5 and 10 _____
8. 4 and 7 _____

The least common multiple is the smallest multiple that two numbers share. Name the least common multiple for each pair of numbers.

9. 3 and 9 ____9____
10. 2 and 9 _____
11. 5 and 6 _____
12. 8 and 10 _____

Underline each complete subject once and circle each simple subject. Underline each complete predicate twice and draw a line through each simple predicate.

13. Carmen walks carefully along the rocky shore.
14. Pools of water collect in rocky crevices near the shore.
15. Tide pools are home to sea plants and animals.
16. Seaweed is the most common tide pool plant.
17. It provides food and shelter for a variety of animals.
18. Carmen sees spiny sea urchins attached to a rock.
19. Their mouths are on their undersides.
20. Their sharp teeth cut seaweed into little pieces.

DAY 13

Language Arts/Algebra

Search for this skill ID on IXL.com for more practice!

A metaphor is a comparison of two different things without using *like* or *as*. A metaphor is an example of figurative language, or language that paints a picture in the reader's mind. Write your own metaphors.

21. People are ___mirrors; you can see yourself in them___.

22. Sleep is _____.

23. Happiness is _____.

24. Life is _____.

25. Friendship is _____.

26. Anger is _____.

Circle the value that makes each equation or inequality true.

27. $x + 12 = 18$
    4, 5, 6

28. $3 \times a = 51$
    15, 17, 21

29. $6 > 3 \times y$
    1, 2, 3

30. $29 < 54 - d$
    20, 25, 28

31. $6 + m = 41$
    25, 35, 45

32. $p - 15 = 19$
    32, 34, 36

33. $8 \times t = 32$
    4, 6, 8

34. $n + 8 > 41$
    23, 28, 38

35. $840 - s = 766$
    64, 74, 78

Let's Play Today *See page 60.

Do push-ups on the ground or against a wall. Count how many you can do in 30 seconds.

Multiplication/Sentence Structure & Types

Rewrite each expression using an exponent. Then, evaluate each expression.

1. $3 \times 3 \times 3 = 3^3 = 27$
2. $2 \times 2 \times 2 \times 2 =$ _____ = _____
3. $8 \times 8 \times 8 =$ _____ = _____
4. $4 \times 4 \times 4 \times 4 \times 4 \times 4 =$ _____ = _____
5. $3 \times 3 \times 3 \times 3 =$ _____ = _____
6. $9 \times 9 \times 9 =$ _____ = _____
7. $10 \times 10 \times 10 \times 10 \times 10 \times 10 \times 10 =$ _____ = _____
8. $5 \times 5 \times 5 \times 5 \times 5 =$ _____ = _____

If the sentence has a compound subject, write *CS* and circle the two simple subjects. If the sentence has a compound predicate, write *CP* and circle the two simple predicates. Write *N* if the sentence has neither a compound subject nor a compound predicate.

9. _____ People have planted crops and raised animals for about 10,000 years.

10. _____ The ancient Chinese and Japanese practiced freshwater and saltwater farming.

11. _____ The Japanese raised oysters as early as 2000 BCE.

12. _____ Fish and shellfish have long been sources of protein for Southeast Asian people.

13. _____ Overfishing and pollution led to the decline of ocean animals over the years.

14. _____ Sea farming and ranching help restore the food supply.

Reading Comprehension

Read the paragraph. Then, answer the questions.

The Trail of Tears

People of different cultures lived in North America before European colonists arrived. As Europeans began to settle in the New World and mine for gold, they competed with Indigenous people for land and other resources. Over time, the New World was divided into states, and a government was formed. The U.S. government passed laws in the 1830s making it legal to force Indigenous people to relocate if colonists wanted their land. The Cherokee and other Indigenous peoples had to move from the southeastern United States to lands farther west. Thousands of Indigenous people traveled more than 1,000 miles (1,600 kilometers) on foot from their homelands to the land that later became the U.S. state of Oklahoma. Many Indigenous people died from disease or hunger along the route. The name Trail of Tears was given to this event in U.S. history because of the struggles people faced on their journeys. Today, the descendants of the survivors of the Trail of Tears make up the Cherokee Nation.

15. What is the main idea of this paragraph?

   A. Many people from Europe settled in the New World.

   B. Some Indigenous people still live in Oklahoma.

   C. The Trail of Tears was the forced relocation of Indigenous people in the United States.

16. What did European colonists compete with Indigenous people for? _____
_____

17. How did the U.S. laws that were passed in the 1830s affect Indigenous people?
_____
_____

18. Where were Indigenous people forced to move? _____
_____

19. What is the Trail of Tears? _____
_____

Parts of Speech/Punctuation

Complete each sentence with an intensive or reflexive pronoun from the word bank.

| himself | yourselves | herself | myself | yourself | ourselves |

1. Mischa isn't home this afternoon, so Nicole will mow the lawn _____ .

2. We were very proud of _____ when the coach handed us the first-place trophy.

3. It is time you took responsibility _____ for your belongings.

4. The judge _____ had tears in his eyes as the jury shared the decision.

5. We want all of you to ask _____ a very important question.

6. I explained the situation to the principal _____ .

A restrictive clause often begins with *that* or *who*. It is needed to make the meaning of the sentence clear. A nonrestrictive clause often begins with *which*. It can be left out and the sentence will still be clear. Nonrestrictive clauses are set off from the rest of the sentence by commas. Read each sentence. If it has a nonrestrictive clause, add commas around it. If it does not, make a check mark on the line.

7. _____ The backpack that I like is on sale.

8. _____ *Wonderama* which came out last summer is Ana's favorite movie.

9. _____ The drawing that was done in charcoal won first prize.

10. _____ The old piano which was badly in need of tuning sat in the corner.

11. _____ The maple tree that has the bright yellow leaves was just a sapling when we moved in.

12. _____ My grandmother attended Hawthorne Elementary which was built in 1928.

Fast Fun Fact

Polar bears' fur isn't actually white. The colorless fur reflects light, which makes it appear white.

Circle the two words that are being compared in each sentence. Then, write *S* if the comparison is a simile. Write *M* if it is a metaphor.

13. _____ The trees are like soldiers standing at attention.

14. _____ When I looked down from the airplane, the cars on the highway were as small as ants.

15. _____ The sound of waves lapping on the shore reminded me of dogs taking a long drink.

16. _____ Twenty circus clowns were like sardines packed in one car.

17. _____ The fans' stomping feet in the bleachers were beating drums.

Most earthquakes occur at plate boundaries. An epicenter is the place on Earth's surface above an earthquake's focus. Study the map of epicenters and answer the questions.

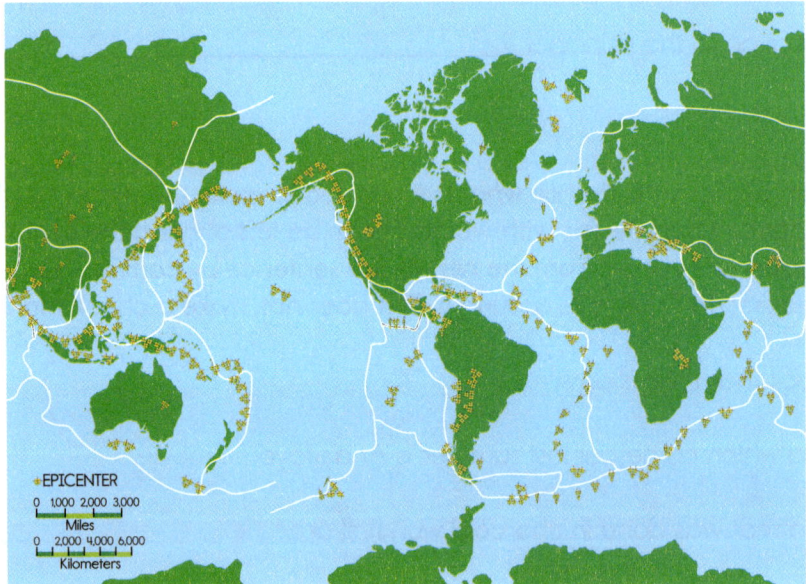

18. Draw a line around the areas with the most earthquake activity.

19. Why do most earthquakes occur at plate boundaries? _____
_____

Numbers/Measurement

Write the next number in each number pattern.

1. 4, 8, 16, 32, 64, _____
2. 1, 4, 7, 6, 9, 12, 11, _____
3. 1, 4, 7, 10, 13, 16, _____
4. 3, 3, 6, 5, 5, 10, 8, 8, 16, 13, 13, _____
5. 3, 5, 8, 12, 17, 23, _____
6. 6, 11, 16, 21, _____
7. 6, 36, 66, 96, _____
8. 1, 5, 9, 8, 12, 16, 15, 19, 23, 22, _____

Find the area of each figure.

> Area of a quadrilateral = length × width
> Area of a triangle = $\frac{1}{2}$ × base × height

9.
5 cm
4 cm
_____ cm²

10.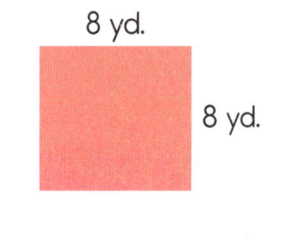
8 yd.
8 yd.
_____ yd.²

11.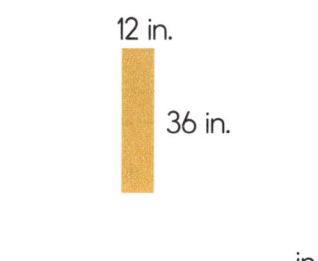
12 in.
36 in.
_____ in.²

12.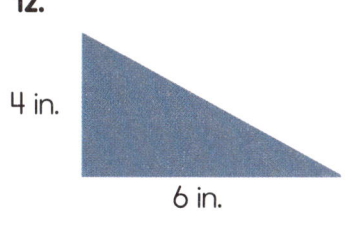
4 in.
6 in.
_____ in.²

13.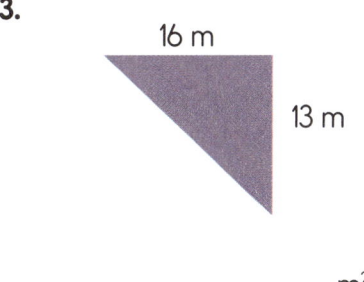
16 m
13 m
_____ m²

14.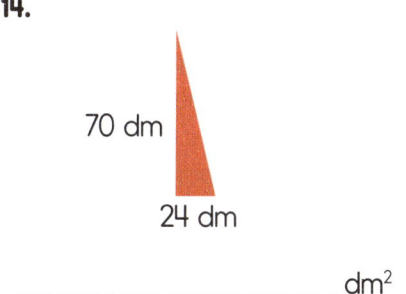
70 dm
24 dm
_____ dm²

Mindful Moment

Think of someone who might need help with something (a friend, family member, or neighbor). Ask them how you can help!

DAY 16

Algebra/Reading Comprehension

Write the missing numbers in each list. Then, write the rule.

15.
M	N
15	20
40	45
90	___
35	___

Rule: M + 5 = N

16.
M	N
25	36
19	30
57	___
___	84

Rule: M + 11 = N

17.
M	N
54	45
89	80
73	___
___	61

Rule: M - _____

18.
M	N
48	37
12	1
___	19
24	___

Rule: _____

19.
M	N
8	48
4	24
10	___
6	___

Rule: _____

20.
M	N
21	7
30	10
18	___
12	___

Rule: _____

Read this part of the U.S. Declaration of Independence. Then, answer the questions.

We hold these truths to be self-evident, that all men are created equal, that they are endowed by their Creator with certain unalienable Rights, that among these are Life, Liberty, and the pursuit of Happiness. —That to secure these rights, Governments are instituted among Men, deriving their just powers from the consent of the governed, — That whenever any Form of Government becomes destructive of these ends, it is the Right of the People to alter or to abolish it, and to institute new Government, laying its foundation on such principles and organizing its powers in such form, as to them shall seem most likely to effect their Safety and Happiness.

21. What are the basic rights of all people according to the Declaration of Independence?
    _____

22. Why are governments "instituted," or created? _____

23. What should people do if they feel the government is not acting in their best interest?
    _____

Multiplication & Division/Parts of Speech

DAY 17

A factor is a divisor of a number. A common factor is a divisor that is shared by two or more numbers. The greatest common factor is the largest common factor shared by two numbers. List the factors for each pair of numbers. Then, circle the greatest common factors.

1. 12: 1, 2, ③, 4, 6, 12
   15: 1, ③, 5, 15

2. 16 _____
   40 _____

3. 9 _____
   12 _____

4. 24 _____
   42 _____

Underline the complete verb and circle the helping verb in each sentence.

5. Jack (was) working in town.

6. Jasmine is walking to the park with her friends.

7. My mother has shopped at that department store for many years.

8. I might have called if I had known you were home.

9. The airport is closed because of yesterday's snowstorm.

10. Hiroto does enjoy sports.

11. Mark is playing outdoors with Sam.

12. Donny does finish his homework every day.

13. Misty and Irmani are watching TV.

Reading Comprehension

Read the paragraph. Then, answer the questions.

The United Nations

The United Nations (UN) is a group of countries that work to promote world peace and good relationships between countries. The UN was formed in 1945, after World War II ended. People from 50 countries went to San Francisco, California, to discuss ways to encourage international cooperation. The UN's Security Council has 15 countries, of which five are permanent members (China, France, the Russian Federation, the United Kingdom, and the United States). These five countries can block proposals brought to the council by voting against them. The other countries on the council are elected to two-year terms. The UN is led by a secretary-general who serves a five-year term. The UN provides peacekeepers to countries at war, helps victims of natural disasters such as flooding, promotes workers' rights, and provides food, medicine, and safe drinking water to those in need. The organization tries to help all people, regardless of where they live.

14. What is the main idea of this paragraph?

    A. The United Nations helps victims of natural disasters.

    B. The United Nations works to promote peace around the world.

    C. The United Nations was formed in 1945.

15. After what world event was the United Nations formed? _____

16. What can the five permanent members of the Security Council do?
    _____

17. How long does the secretary-general serve? _____

18. What are three ways that the United Nations helps people around the world?
    _____
    _____
    _____

Fractions/Sentence Structure

Express each as a ratio in simplest form.

1. There are 4 green marbles and 8 red marbles in a bag. Write the ratio of green marbles to red marbles.

    $\frac{4}{8} = \frac{1}{2}$

2. There are 12 cars and 3 motorcycles in a parking lot. Write the ratio of cars to motorcycles.

    _____

3. There are 10 soccer balls and 15 footballs in a storeroom. Write the ratio of soccer balls to footballs.

    _____

4. There are 11 dogs and 4 cats at a kennel. Write the ratio of dogs to cats.

    _____

5. There are 8 quarters and 3 dimes in a coin purse. Write the ratio of quarters to dimes.

    _____

6. There are 12 robins and 15 chickadees in a tree. Write the ratio of robins to chickadees.

    _____

Combine each pair of sentences to write a compound sentence using *and* or *but*. In each new sentence, place a comma before the conjunction.

7. The frogs sleep during the day. They hunt for food at night.

    _____

    _____

8. A parrot's bright colors are easy to see in a tree. A tree boa's green color makes it difficult to spot.

    _____

    _____

9. A fruit bat has a long nose. It has large eyes to help it see in the dark.

    _____

    _____

Language Arts/Science

An idiom is a phrase that states one thing but means another. Draw a line to match each idiom with its meaning.

10. I can do math problems standing on my head. — Who told the secret?

11. Who let the cat out of the bag? — She will sleep very well tonight.

12. Charlie is a chip off the old block. — I know math well.

13. Jenna will sleep like a log. — The two friends are very similar.

14. Cora and Alexis are like two peas in a pod. — He is just like his father.

Write *T* for true or *F* for false for each statement. Use an online resource for help if needed.

15. _____ A volcano is an opening in Earth's crust through which lava, gases, ash, and rocks erupt.

16. _____ Volcanic material can build up to form mountains.

17. _____ These mountains can form only on land.

18. _____ All magma comes from Earth's core.

19. _____ Most volcanoes happen underwater.

20. _____ Most volcanoes on land occur at diverging plate boundaries.

Let's Play Today * See page 60.

Squatting down on your hands and feet like a frog, hop around inside your home or outside in an open space.

© Carson Dellosa Education

Multiplication

DAY 19

The distributive property states: $a \times (b + c) = (a \times b) + (a \times c)$. The same property also means that: $a \times (b - c) = (a \times b) - (a \times c)$. The distributive property can help simplify complex math problems. Rewrite each expression using the distributive property. Then, solve.

1. $21 \times 13 =$ $(21 \times 10) + (21 \times 3) = 210 + 63$ = 273
2. $12 \times 55 =$ _____ = _____
3. $61 \times 15 =$ _____ = _____
4. $45 \times 22 =$ _____ = _____
5. $16 \times 47 =$ _____ = _____
6. $37 \times 102 =$ _____ = _____
7. $64 \times 13 =$ _____ = _____
8. $48 \times 44 =$ _____ = _____
9. $33 \times 32 =$ _____ = _____

10. There are 18 spots on each ladybug. How many total spots are there on 12 ladybugs?

11. Each plane taxiing to leave has 210 passengers on board. How many passengers are there if 5 planes are taxiing to leave?

12. Juwan counts 18 stars in the sky every night for a whole week. How many stars does he count for all 7 nights?

13. A landscaping company ordered 54 saplings to plant. If each sapling cost $89, how much did the landscaping company pay for all of the saplings?

DAY 19

Search for this skill ID on IXL.com for more practice!

Language Arts/Writing

Choose the correct meaning of the bold idiom in each sentence.

14. She is a **big cheese** at her school.
    A. cafeteria worker
    B. principal
    C. very important person

15. My dad is the **top dog** at his job.
    A. loudest one
    B. parts supplier
    C. one in charge; boss

16. After working all afternoon in the yard, Grandma and I decided to **call it a day** and go to dinner.
    A. stop
    B. talk
    C. rake leaves

17. She did not talk about her family because she did not want to reveal the **skeletons in her closet**.
    A. her family secrets
    B. where she kept trash
    C. the end of a scary story

18. Linh would give you **the shirt off his back** if necessary.
    A. lend you a shirt
    B. help any way he could
    C. keep you warm

19. Maria had the answer to Connor's question on the **tip of her tongue**.
    A. unable to think of the answer
    B. could not talk
    C. about to be remembered

If you could live in one time period in history, which period would you choose? Why? What do you think your life would be like on a daily basis? (What would you wear? What would you eat? What would you do for fun?) Write a paragraph about your life in that time period.

_____
_____
_____
_____
_____
_____

Algebra/Vocabulary

Translate each description into an algebraic expression. Then, evaluate the expression using the value shown in the box for the variable.

| $a = 3$ | $b = 2$ | $c = 5$ | $d = 7$ |
| $w = 1$ | $x = 12$ | $y = 9$ | $z = 4$ |

1. the product of 3 and a added to 12 = __(3 × a) + 12__ = __21__ when __a = 3__

2. y times 12 = _____ = ____ when _____

3. the quotient of 36 and b _____ = ____ when _____

4. 14 added to w _____ = ____ when _____

5. the product of z and 6 divided by 12 _____ = ____ when _____

6. c to the second power times 2 _____ = ____ when _____

7. the difference of d and 15 divided by 4 _____ = ____ when _____

8. 23 added to the quotient of x and 6 _____ = ____ when _____

Fill in the spaces in the table below.

Word	Latin or Greek Root	Root's Meaning
thermostat		
	bi	two
meteorology		
	rupt	
monarchy		
pedestrian		foot

Read the paragraph. Then, answer the questions.

Meteorologists

Most people have seen weather forecasters on TV. People who study the weather are called *meteorologists*. Most of their jobs are performed off camera in offices or laboratories where they study the weather. Meteorologists study past weather patterns to help them predict future weather. They take readings of temperature, wind speed, atmospheric pressure, and precipitation (rain or snow) to forecast the weather. They may use satellites, airplanes, and weather balloons to collect additional data. Meteorologists develop computer models to predict how climate and weather might change in the future. They also study how weather phenomena, such as tornadoes, form. An important part of a meteorologist's job is giving people accurate information in case of an emergency. If your community is being threatened by a storm, such as a hurricane, you need to know when it might strike and how to stay safe.

9. What is the main idea of this paragraph?

    A. Weather forecasters often appear on TV.

    B. Tornadoes and hurricanes can cause great damage.

    C. Meteorologists study the weather.

10. Why do meteorologists study weather patterns of the past? _____
_____

11. What does a meteorologist consider when forecasting the weather? _____
_____
_____

12. How can computer models help? _____
_____

13. What might a meteorologist tell you about a hurricane? _____
_____

Fast Fun Fact

An extreme heat wave can make train tracks bend.

© Carson Dellosa Education

Science Experiment

Paper Airplane

The paper airplane you will create in this activity demonstrates the movement of an airplane in response to the air through which it is traveling. If you work on your design carefully, you can get your airplane to soar like an eagle!

Materials
- sheet of paper (8 $\frac{1}{2}$" x 11")
- scissors
- tape

Procedure

1. Fold the upper edge of the paper to the opposite side of the paper. (A) Unfold and repeat with the other side. You should now have an X on your page. Fold the top to the bottom of the X created by the first two folds. (B)
2. Fold in the middle crease on both sides, bringing the top corners toward the bottom of the X. Now, the paper should look like a house. (C)
3. Fold the tip of the roof to the gutter. (D)
4. Fold the airplane in half so that the folds are not showing. (E)
5. Fold down the wings. The body of the airplane should be no more than a half inch (1.27 cm) tall. (F)
6. Fold the outer quarter inch (0.635 cm) of the airplane wing. Tape the two wings together at the middle fold. (G)
7. Cut two small flaps in the back of the wings in the sections illustrated. These will help direct the movement of the airplane. (G)
8. By bending the flaps on the back of the wing, you can get the airplane to bank either left or right. If you bend both flaps the same way, you can get the airplane to climb sharply into the air.

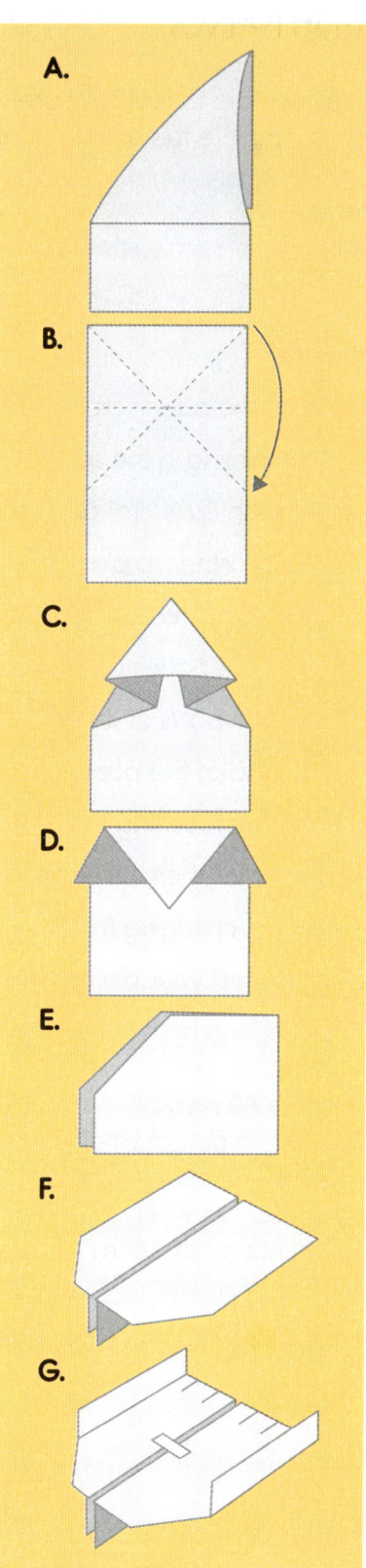

Search for this skill ID on IXL.com for more practice!

Science Experiment

Human Nerves

People are able to feel because we have nerves. Some places in our bodies have more nerves than others. Complete this activity to see which places have more nerves and are more sensitive.

Materials
- partner
- paper clip

Procedure

1. Open the paper clip so that the two endpoints are pointing in the same direction, at least one inch (2.54 cm) apart.
2. Ask a partner to place their arm on a table and close their eyes. You will touch the paper clip's endpoints to different parts of their fingers and arm to see if they can tell whether you are using one end of the paper clip or two.
3. Begin by touching their fingertips with two endpoints. Ask them if they feel one or two points. Tell them whether they are correct or incorrect. Repeat with several different fingers, changing from one to two points and back again.
4. Slowly test your partner's nerves by touching the points to their mid-fingers, palms, wrists, and both sides of the forearm. Change from one to two points at random.

What's This All About?
Nerves, which detect when a body part is touched, are distributed all over the human body. However, nerves are not distributed evenly. By finding out where your partner can feel both ends of the paper clip, you also find out where the body's nerves are closest together. What do you notice about the function of the body parts that seem to have a lot of nerves?

Social Studies Activity

The Mayflower Compact

Read the passage. Then, circle *fact* or *opinion* for each statement.

    The Pilgrims were a group of people who disagreed with how the Church of England was run. They wanted to go to a place where they could establish their own church. They received permission to travel to Virginia, where they could worship as they pleased. In September of 1620, about 50 Pilgrims and 50 other English people (whom the Pilgrims called "Strangers") set sail for America on a ship called the *Mayflower*. In November of 1620, the ship arrived at Cape Cod in present-day Massachusetts. The water to the south was too rough and dangerous, so they decided to colonize that area of Massachusetts, an area already inhabited by Indigenous people.

    Because the trip had not turned out as planned, some of the Strangers talked about leaving the group. However, the group believed that they had a better chance for survival if they all stuck together, and they had a better chance of sticking together if they agreed at the start to follow certain rules. They wrote an agreement called the *Mayflower Compact*. Many people consider the Mayflower Compact to be the first form of self-government in America's history. The document declared that the group would stay together and form their own laws and government. All who signed promised to follow these laws. Forty-one men signed the compact. Women and Indigenous people were not allowed to sign it. They elected John Carver as their first governor and set out to look for fresh water. After exploring the area, they decided to colonize nearby Plymouth.

1. The Pilgrims' ideas about the church were better than England's ideas.   fact   opinion

2. The *Mayflower* sailed in 1620.   fact   opinion

3. Signing the Mayflower Compact was a good idea.   fact   opinion

4. Forty-one men signed the Mayflower Compact.   fact   opinion

5. John Carver was the smartest person on the *Mayflower*.   fact   opinion

6. About 100 people traveled to America on the *Mayflower*.   fact   opinion

7. The *Mayflower* did not land where the Pilgrims had planned.   fact   opinion

8. The Mayflower Compact was a perfect agreement.   fact   opinion

The Branches of the U.S. Government

Write the name of the U.S. branch of government (*legislative*, *executive*, or *judicial*) for each responsibility.

1. can impeach the president   _____

2. writes bills   _____

3. approves or vetoes bills   _____

4. interprets and examines laws   _____

5. appoints justices   _____

The U.S. government is divided into three branches. Each branch is given different but equal powers. Write the responsibilities of each branch in the pie chart. With an adult, use the Internet for help.

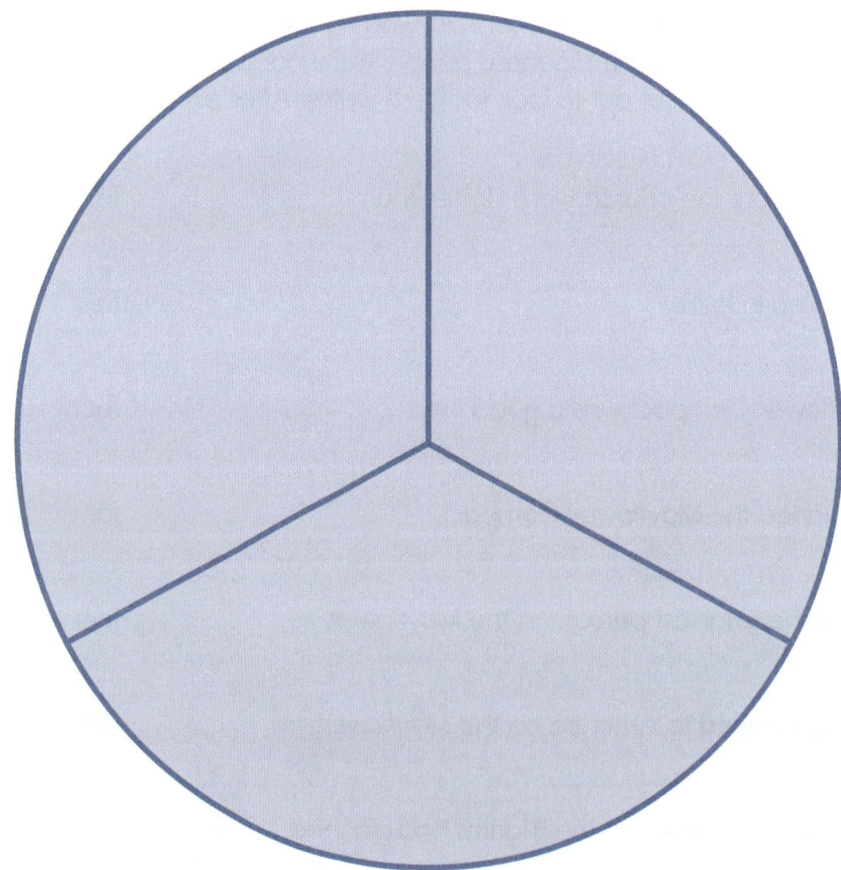

Social Studies Activity

Reading Rainfall Maps

Precipitation maps, or rainfall maps, use patterns to show areas with varying amounts of rainfall or snow. Compare the precipitation maps of the main island of Hawaii and Arizona.

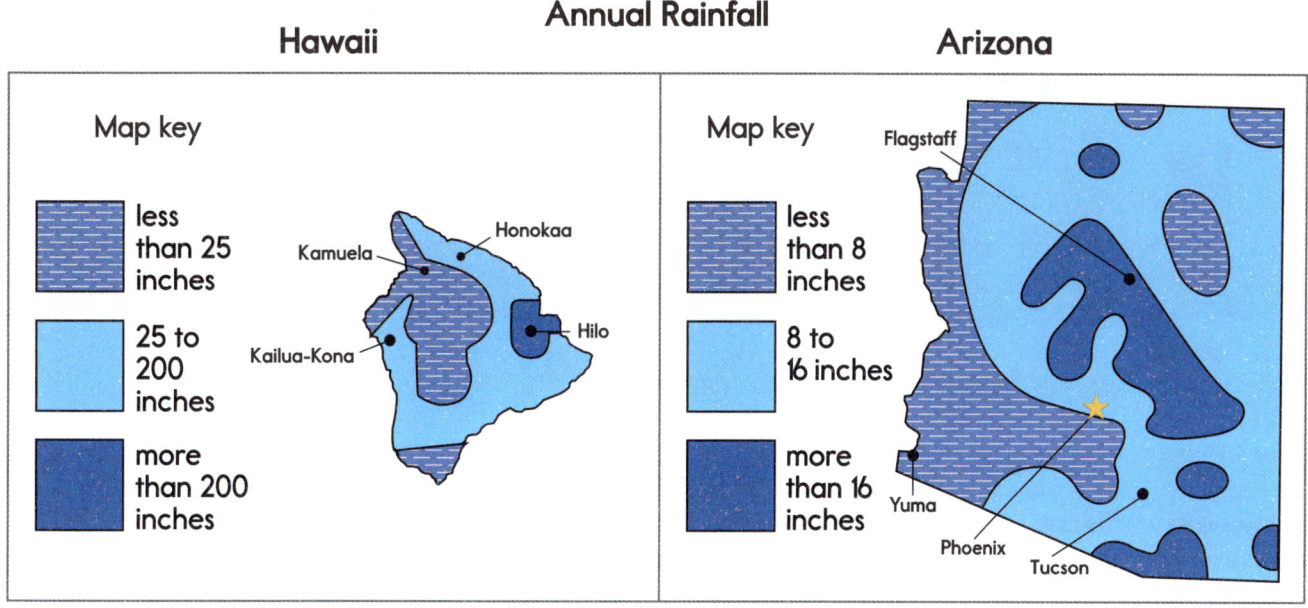

1. Which state receives more rainfall? _____

2. How much annual rainfall does Hilo, Hawaii, receive? _____

3. What does ▒ on the Arizona map represent? _____

4. What does ■ on the Hawaii map represent? _____

5. Which city is in the driest area in Hawaii? _____

6. Which city on the Arizona map receives the most rainfall? _____

7. Which two cities in Arizona receive 8 to 16 inches (20.32 to 40.64 cm) of rain annually?

   _____ and _____

8. Which two cities in Hawaii receive 25 to 200 inches (63.5 to 508 cm) of rain annually?

   _____ and _____

SECTION 3

Monthly Goals

Think of three goals to set for yourself this month. For example, you may want to learn five new vocabulary words each week. Write your goals on the lines. Post them someplace visible, where you will see them every day.

Draw a line through each goal as you meet it. Feel proud that you have met your goals and set new ones to continue to challenge yourself.

1. _____
2. _____
3. _____

Word List

The following words are used in this section. Use a dictionary to look up each word that you do not know. Write three sentences. Use a word from the word list in each sentence.

attire   prestigious
gigantic   punctual
hazardous   revolution
median   sapling
ornately   Shoshone

1. _____
   _____
2. _____
   _____
3. _____
   _____

Introduction to Endurance

This section includes Let's Play Today and Mindful Moments activities that focus on endurance. These activities are designed to help you develop mental and physical stamina. If you have limited mobility, feel free to modify any suggested activity or choose a different one from the list on the following page.

Let's Play Today

Many children seem to have endless energy and can run, jump, and play for hours. But endurance does not come naturally to everyone. Developing endurance requires regular exercise that gets the body moving and the heart pumping, like arm punches, jumping jacks, dancing, and playing sports.

Make exercise a part of your everyday routine during the summer. Do things that make you breathe harder and move your body, such as playing tag, going for a walk, kicking a ball with someone, swimming, riding a bike, and more.

Mindful Moments

Endurance means to stick with something, and it applies to the mind as well as to the body. If you have ever felt like giving up at something but instead you persevered and finished the task, you demonstrated endurance.

Think of a time when you wanted to quit a task. Maybe you didn't like the new game you were playing or the new skill you were practicing, and so you wanted to quit. What did you do? Realize that it often takes a while to learn something new. If you quit instead of persevering through a challenge, you wouldn't learn how to do new things and you wouldn't grow as a person. Endurance and perseverance build character and make people mentally strong. Quitting should be a last resort. Developing endurance at a young age will help you persevere through challenging physical and mental activities you encounter in life.

Engaging Online Practice

Bring learning to life with fun, interactive activities on IXL! Look for the Skill ID box and type the 3-digit code into the search bar on IXL.com or the IXL mobile app. Ten questions per day are free!

Skill IDs
5UN • D9K

SECTION 3

Let's Play Today

Get up and moving with these Let's Play Today activities. Section 3 focuses on endurance. Endurance is being able to complete many repetitions of a task, such as 10 jumping jacks, or perform an activity for an extended amount of time, such as riding a bike for 10 minutes. Building endurance will help you get through everyday tasks and find success with physical activities and sports. Use this list in addition to or as a replacement for any Let's Play Today suggestions on the activity pages. This list was developed to be inclusive of a variety of abilities. Choose the ones that are a good fit for you! Make modifications as needed. These activities may require adult supervision. See page 2 for full caution information.

Jump Rope:
Start by jumping rope for 30 seconds. Jump rope every day and try to increase the amount of time you can jump every day.

Freeze Dance:
Have one person control the music. Ask them to play a favorite song. Dance while the music plays. When the music pauses, stop dancing. If you dance after the music stops, the person controlling the music assigns an endurance challenge (5 jumping jacks, push-ups, etc.). Then you can rejoin the game.

Scavenger Hunt Hike:
Go on a scavenger hunt hike. Create a list of things you think you might see, such as a traffic light, a dog, or a particular type of flower. Cross items off your list as you go. You can also build endurance by going on a simple walk or run.

Fun on Wheels:
Go on a bike ride or play bike games. This works great with wheelchairs too. Create an obstacle course of cones and weave in and out, challenge a friend to a race, or use chalk to create roads, stop signs, and more.

Let's Go Team:
Playing team sports is a great way to build endurance. Basketball, soccer, football, softball, baseball, volleyball, and more are all great ways to improve endurance. Choose a favorite team sport and get a group of kids together to play at a local park.

Measurement/Grammar

Find the area of each figure.

The area of a parallelogram = base × height.

1.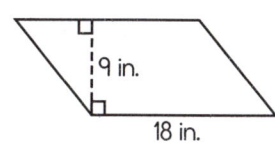

   A = _____ sq. in.

2.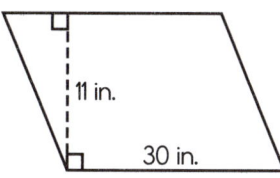

   A = _____ sq. in.

3.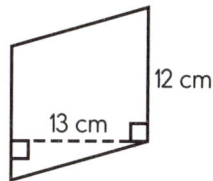

   A = _____ sq. cm

To find the area of an irregular shape, separate the shape into two or more smaller figures. Find the area of each part and then add them together.

4.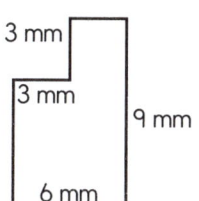

   A = _____ sq. mm

5.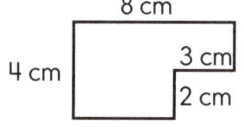

   A = _____ sq. cm

6.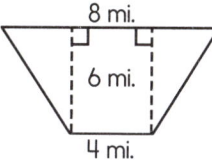

   A = _____ sq. mi.

Write *I* or *me* to correctly complete each sentence.

7. Mom and _____ went to the store.

8. Will you come to see Joon and _____?

9. Ann Marie and _____ ate our lunches outside.

Circle the possessive pronoun that correctly completes each sentence.

10. (Her, hers) handwriting is very neat.

11. The prize is (his, our).

12. The book you loaned to Leza was (my, mine).

Numbers/Reading Comprehension

A negative number is a number that has a value of less than zero. A positive number is a number that is greater than zero. Write the negative numbers on the number line.

13.

Read the passage. Then, answer the questions.

Sacagawea

A U.S. gold dollar coin shows the image of a young Indigenous woman named Sacagawea and her baby. In 1800, when Sacagawea was about 12 years old, an enemy tribe captured her. They took her far away from her Shoshone home. Four years later, Sacagawea joined a group of explorers who wanted to find a way to the Pacific Ocean. Meriwether Lewis and William Clark would lead the group across the American Northwest. Sacagawea went with her husband. Her baby son was strapped to her back. She was the only woman in the group of explorers.

Sacagawea helped make the trip a success. In May of 1805, she jumped into the river to save the explorers' journals that had fallen out of the canoe. Sacagawea found edible plants for the men and acted as interpreter when they met different Indigenous peoples. In August of 1805, the explorers came upon a group of Shoshones. The chief was Sacagawea's brother, whom she had not seen in five years. The tribe gave the explorers the food, guides, and horses they needed to finish their journey and to return home safely. Sacagawea had helped them greatly.

14. What is the main idea of the second paragraph?

   A. Sacagawea helped the explorers survive.

   B. The explorers made discoveries during exploration.

   C. Sacagawea saw the Pacific Ocean.

15. What area did Lewis and Clark plan to explore? _____

Mindful Moment

Experience the world around you using your senses. Notice 5 things you can see, 4 things you can feel, 3 things you can hear, 2 things you can smell, and 1 thing you can taste.

Parts of Speech/Numbers

DAY 2

A pronoun that is part of the subject of a sentence is called a subject pronoun. A pronoun that is not part of the subject is an object pronoun. Write *SP* if the underlined pronoun is a subject pronoun. Write *OP* if it is an object pronoun.

1. _____ The funny story made <u>us</u> laugh.
2. _____ Did <u>they</u> fly or take the train home?
3. _____ Ted held the trophy in front of McCall and <u>her</u>.
4. _____ <u>We</u> are going to Maine this summer.
5. _____ Will <u>we</u> see any sharks at Sea Life Park?
6. _____ Are <u>you</u> a cousin of Hal Tomyn?
7. _____ Suki and <u>I</u> went ice-skating with her family.
8. _____ The dog found <u>it</u> under the kitchen table.
9. _____ Do not give <u>her</u> the present until noon.
10. _____ <u>I</u> bought blue gym shoes this year.

The absolute value of a number is its distance from zero on a number line. Absolute value is shown by vertical lines on either side of an integer. Write the absolute value of each integer.

11. |8| __8__
12. |-8| __8__
13. |12| _____
14. |-7| _____
15. |15| _____
16. |23| _____
17. |-105| _____
18. |48| _____
19. |-17| _____
20. |-3| _____
21. |62| _____
22. |-14| _____
23. |-29| _____
24. |82| _____

Language Arts/Writing

Look up the word *dramatize* in a dictionary. Then, answer the questions.

25. What are the guide words on the page? _____

26. How many meanings are listed for *dramatize*? _____

27. Write the word. Write the pronunciation. _____

28. How many syllables does the word have? _____

29. What does *dramatize* mean in this sentence: Do you always have to *dramatize*, Annie?
_____

30. Write the other forms of the word given in the dictionary and tell what part(s) of

    speech they are. _____

31. List two words on the same page as *dramatize*. Write their pronunciations.

_____

Pretend that you live in the year 2050. What will life be like? How will it be different from life today? Write a detailed paragraph and draw a picture on a separate sheet of paper to describe and show what you imagine.

_____

_____

_____

_____

_____

_____

_____

Fractions/Vocabulary

IXL Skill IDs: JSZ • FSZ

DAY 3

In each situation, find the rate.

1. You drive 220 miles in 4 hours. What is the rate per hour?

   _____

2. Your heart beats 234 times each minute. What is the rate per second?

   _____

3. It snows 3 inches in 4 hours. What is the rate per hour?

   _____

4. You spend $3.40 for a 20-ounce box of cereal. What is the rate per ounce?

   _____

5. You consume 13,300 calories in 7 days. What is the rate per day?

   _____

6. You spend $2.25 for a 0.5-gallon container of frozen yogurt. What is the rate per gallon?

   _____

Circle the correct meaning for each root word. Then, write two words that contain that root.

7. chron   A. time   B. fear   C. study of

   _____   _____

8. astr   A. life   B. stars   C. earth

   _____   _____

9. path   A. feeling   B. fear   C. small

   _____   _____

10. bio   A. sea   B. pull   C. life

    _____   _____

Let's Play Today *See page 108.*

Lying on the ground with your legs in the air, pretend you're pedaling a bicycle. Time yourself to see how long you can pedal.

© Carson Dellosa Education

The Post Office

In the United States and Canada, the post office is where people buy stamps and mail letters and packages. Postal employees sort mail by region and send it out for delivery on foot, by car, by truck, or by airplane. A country's national post office sets the rates for mailing materials. The cost of postage depends on the size and weight of an item, the distance to its destination, and its target delivery date. Sending the items to arrive the next day costs more than sending them by general delivery, which may take days or weeks. Some post offices offer services such as processing passport applications, banking, and selling greeting cards. Canada Post, the postal service in Canada, is run by the government. The U.S. Postal Service is part of the executive branch of the government but is run independently. Both government postal organizations face competition from private postal companies that may offer faster mail delivery at a lower cost.

11. What is the main idea of this paragraph?
    A. Mail is sorted by region.
    B. The Canadian postal service is called Canada Post.
    C. The post office is important for communicating by mail.

12. Why do people visit post offices? _____

13. How do postal employees transport mail? _____

14. Who determines the rates for mailing materials? _____

15. What does the cost of postage depend on? _____

Algebra/Sentence Structure

Equivalent expressions are created by simplifying values and combining terms. If the expression includes exponents, calculate the values before simplifying: $3^2 = 9$. If the expression contains repeated addition, use multiplication instead: $x + x + x = 3x$. Create equivalent expressions.

1. $3(12x + 5) =$ __36x + 15__

2. $12(5y - 3) =$ _____

3. $2^3(5g + 2) =$ _____

4. $x(x + 8) =$ _____

5. $25(3 - 4n) =$ _____

6. $8(z + z + z + z) =$ _____

7. $4^2(2x + 4) - 12 =$ _____

8. $5(3y + 13) =$ _____

9. $4(2w^2 - 4) =$ _____

10. $15(3c - 2) =$ _____

11. $6(k + k + k - 7) =$ _____

12. $12 \div (a + a + a) =$ _____

Writing is more interesting when a variety of sentence structures are used. Write a sentence to fit each description.

13. Write a sentence with a simple subject and simple predicate with adjectives, articles, and adverbs.

    _____

14. Write a sentence with a direct object and an indirect object.

    _____

15. Write a sentence with two prepositional phrases.

    _____

16. Write a sentence with a compound subject and/or verb.

    _____

DAY 4

Vocabulary

Write *yes* or *no* to answer each question. Use a dictionary if you need help.

17. Would a boy wear a *mukluk*? _____

18. Could you work as a *gofer*? _____

19. Do you wear a *goatee* on your arm? _____

20. Could you play with a *googol*? _____

21. Is a *truffle* a rich chocolate candy? _____

22. Could you plant a *vetch*? _____

23. Does *yep* mean yes? _____

24. Is a *yeti* mysterious? _____

25. Could animals be kept in a *scribe*? _____

26. Is an *orlop* deck part of a ship? _____

27. Would you chop wood with an *italic*? _____

28. Can you drive an *osier*? _____

Choose two vocabulary words from above. Use each one correctly in a sentence. Circle the word in each sentence.

29. _____

_____

30. _____

_____

116   © Carson Dellosa Education

Algebra/Vocabulary  DAY 5

A number line can be used to represent the possible values of a variable. In the first problem, the open circle shows that the values do not include 8. For inequalities that use ≥ (greater than or equal to) or ≤ (less than or equal to), a closed circle indicates that the values do include that point. Solve each inequality. Represent the possible values of the variable using the number line.

1. $x > 3 + 5$

2. $y - 7 < -3$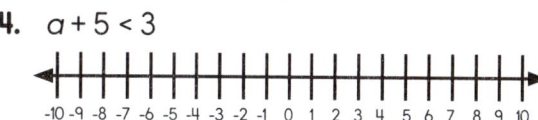

3. $d + 10 \geq 9$

4. $a + 5 < 3$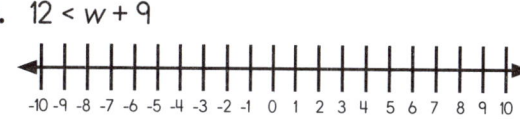

5. $7 + c \leq -1$

6. $12 < w + 9$

Many words have denotations (definitions) as well as connotations (feelings and values associated with the word). For example, the denotation of both *clever* and *shrewd* is "smart." However, *clever* has a more positive connotation, while *shrewd* has a more negative connotation. Match each word with another word that has a similar denotation but different connotation. Write the letter of the matching word on the line.

| A. scent | B. request | C. depart | D. stingy |
| E. hungry | F. unique | G. mutt | H. immature |

7. _____ thrifty   8. _____ childlike   9. _____ odor

10. _____ odd   11. _____ dog   12. _____ escape

13. _____ starving   14. _____ demand

 **Fast Fun Fact**

Since every gorilla has a unique wrinkle pattern on its nose, conservation workers use these "nose prints" to identify them.

Search for this skill ID on IXL.com for more practice!

Vocabulary/Data Analysis

Write an *X* beside the word or phrase that is a synonym for the bold word. Use a thesaurus if you need help.

15. **bronco**

_____ panther

_____ horse

_____ insect

16. **fanfare**

_____ explanation

_____ metal

_____ music

17. **residence**

_____ payment

_____ home

_____ disease

18. **narrative**

_____ complaint

_____ length

_____ story

19. **sapling**

_____ young plant

_____ vitamin

_____ young tree

20. **attire**

_____ medal

_____ wisdom

_____ clothing

- The *range* is the difference between the highest and lowest numbers in a set of data.
- To calculate the *mean* (or average), add the list of numbers and divide by the number of items.
- The *median* is the middle number that appears in the data when it is arranged in numeric order.
- The *mode* is the number that appears most often in the data.

Use the chart to answer the questions about the number of medals awarded at a recent Olympic Games.

21. What is the range of the data?

_____

22. What is the mode of the data?

_____

23. What is the median of the data?

_____

24. What is the mean number of medals awarded? _____

Country	Number of Medals
United States	91
Russia	88
China	59
Australia	58
Germany	56
Italy	34
Cuba	29
Great Britain	28
South Korea	28

Fractions/Problem Solving

Use equal ratios to solve each problem.

1. The Dollar-Mart grocery store sells 6 bars of soap for $1.00. How many bars of soap can a customer buy with $9.00?

2. Kelsey's soccer team scored 5 points in 2 games. At this rate, how many points will the team score in 16 games?

3. The O'Neil family is driving 60 miles per hour. If they continue to drive at this speed, how many miles will they drive in 4 hours?

Complete the table.

	Regular Price	Discount Rate	Discount	Sale Price
4.	$24	40%		
5.	$25	30%		
6.	$80	15%		
7.	$220	60%		
8.	$90	55%		
9.	$120	45%		
10.	$1,250	25%		

Reading Comprehension

Read the paragraph. Then, answer the questions.

North American Pioneers

Many early North American colonists came from Europe. Some came to pursue religious freedom, while others wanted more land for their families. Many colonists built villages along the shores of lakes, rivers, and the ocean. Water was important, not only for drinking, farming, and washing clothes, but also for powering mills and traveling to other areas. Most colonists worked as farmers. They had to clear the land of trees before they could plant many crops. Colonists also raised horses and oxen to help pull wagons and sheep to provide wool. When there were enough children in a village, parents sometimes built a schoolhouse and hired a teacher. Usually, all of the children were taught in a single room. Otherwise, children might be educated at home. As villages grew in size, they sometimes built a doctor's office, a blacksmith's shop, and a general store where goods were sold.

11. What is the main idea of this paragraph?
    A. Some colonists came from Europe.
    B. Colonists' children sometimes studied at home.
    C. Most early colonists were farmers who lived in small villages.

12. Why did the early colonists come to North America? _____

13. Which animals did colonists often raise? _____

14. How were colonists' children educated? _____

15. What other buildings might a colonist village include? _____

Mindful Moment

On a piece of paper, finish this sentence:
"One thing that always makes me laugh or smile is . . ." Write about it.

Measurement/Language Arts

Convert each measurement.

> 12 inches (in.) = 1 foot (ft.)
> 3 ft. = 1 yard (yd.)

1. 12 in. = _____ ft.
2. 18 in. = _____ ft.
3. 2 ft. = _____ in.
4. 48 in. = _____ ft.
5. 6 ft. = _____ yd.
6. 7 yd. = _____ ft.
7. 1 yd. = _____ in.
8. 9 ft. = _____ yd.
9. 3 yd. = _____ ft.

Each sentence contains informal language. Read the sentence carefully and then rewrite it on the line using more formal English.

10. "I thought the concert was totally off the hook," said Marissa.

    _____

11. That construction across the street is really driving me nuts.

    _____

12. Thanks a bunch for filling me in about what's going on.

    _____

13. We've only got a few minutes before the bell, so you've got to get it done ASAP.

    _____

    _____

14. Anyways, there was this humungous traffic jam that held things up forever.

    _____

    _____

15. "Chill out," said Jaxson, "we have 20 minutes before the bell rings."

    _____

Language Arts

Read the partial table of contents and index from a history book. Then, answer the questions.

Table of Contents

Chapter Five
The Nation Grows 216
Exploring the West 217
Louisiana Purchase 222
War of 1812 229
Country Growth 236

Chapter Six
The Civil War 250
The Beginning 251
The Two Sides 260
The First Part of the War 270
The Second Part 289
The Civil War at Sea 300

Maps R60
Glossary R95

Index

Civil War 250-300
    conflict over slavery 254-293
    Reconstruction 294-300
Economy 97, 319, 420
    after American Revolution 97-100
    after Civil War 319
    of Great Lakes 420

Jackson, Andrew 100-101, 124-130
Louisiana Purchase 222
Massasoit 172
Native Americans
    (see Indigenous people)
Waterloo 5-6, 12, 21-25, 610

16. What is the difference between the table of contents and the index in a book?

_____

_____

17. If you wanted to see if there was a picture of Andrew Jackson in the book, where would you look?

_____

18. Where would you look to find out who fought in the Civil War? _____

_____

19. How many sections are in Chapter Five? _____

20. On what page could you look to learn who Massasoit was? _____

Measurement/Reading Comprehension

Convert each measurement.

1 kilometer (km) = 1,000 meters (m)	10 dm = 100 centimeters (cm)
1 m = 10 decimeters (dm)	100 cm = 1,000 millimeters (mm)

1. 25 cm = _____ mm
2. 3 m = _____ mm
3. 9 dm = _____ mm
4. 10 dm = _____ mm
5. 12 m = _____ mm
6. 8 m = _____ cm
7. 50 mm = _____ cm
8. 100 m = _____ cm
9. 4 km = _____ cm

Choose a fiction book from the library, your home, or the Summer Reading List from the QR code on page 8. Describe how the author develops the point of view of the narrator. Does the reader know everything the narrator thinks and feels? How does the narrator's point of view shape the story?

_____
_____
_____
_____
_____
_____
_____
_____
_____

Let's Play Today *See page 108.*

Jump rope! Time yourself to see for how long you can jump.

DAY 8

 Reading Comprehension/Geometry

Read the following passage. Then, answer the questions.

Timbuktu

Timbuktu is a small trading town in central Mali, located near the southern edge of the Sahara Desert. Established around 1100 CE, it was a trading post for products from North and West Africa. Northern camel caravans traded salt, cloth, cowrie shells, and copper for gold, kola nuts, ivory, and enslaved people who came from the South.

Timbuktu's location left it open to attack, and control of the city changed many times. It has been ruled by the Mali Empire, the Songhai Empire, Morocco, nomads, France, and others. It is not as important or populated as it once was. Many of its mud and brick buildings are eroding and are half-buried in the sand.

10. Underline the topic sentence of the passage.

11. Circle the main idea of the first paragraph.

12. Circle the main idea of the second paragraph.

To find the surface area of a rectangular prism, first find the area of each side. Then, add to find the sum. Find the surface area of each figure.

13.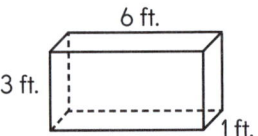

surface area = _____ square feet

14.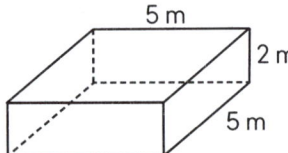

surface area = _____ square meters

15.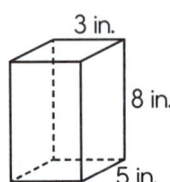

surface area = _____ square inches

16.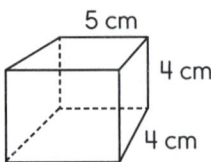

surface area = _____ square centimeters

Measurement/Capitalization & Punctuation

Convert each measurement.

16 ounces (oz.) = 1 pound (lb.)
2,000 lb. = 1 ton (T)

2 cups = 1 pint (pt.)
2 pt. = 1 quart (qt.)
8 pt. = 1 gallon (gal.)

1. 32 oz. = _____ lb.
2. 3 lb. = _____ oz.
3. 1 ton = _____ lb.
4. 4,000 lb. = _____ tons
5. 2 cups = _____ pt.
6. 3 pt. = _____ cups
7. 2 pt. = _____ qt.
8. 8 pt. = _____ gal.
9. 1 cup = _____ gal.

Rewrite the friendly letter. Use the correct form, punctuation marks, and capitalization. Be sure to indent each paragraph.

1624 bay lane short creek pa 12525 may 10 2024 dear aunt ann and uncle jamal school will soon be out for the summer i am looking forward to it the year was good and i learned a lot mom and dad are going to france in july i don't want to go with them I'm writing this letter to ask if i can stay with you july 10 through July 22 i would love to help you take care of the horses and do anything else that you would want me to do i would also help around the house please let me know if i can come your loving niece julie ann

_____
_____
_____
_____
_____
_____
_____
_____
_____

Reading Comprehension

Read the passage. Then, answer the questions.

Gwendolyn Brooks

Gwendolyn Brooks began writing poems when she was seven years old. When her parents saw how much she loved to work with words, they set up a desk for her and told her that she could write instead of doing chores in the house.

Brooks liked to write about families like hers. She wrote about people who lived in the city and sometimes struggled to afford food to eat. But these people were happy and loved life.

By the age of 16, Brooks had published 75 poems. At 25, she won her first writing award. She published her first book of poems, *A Street in Bronzeville*, in 1945. It contained poems about people who lived in the part of Chicago, Illinois, where Brooks lived.

In 1949, Brooks published *Annie Allen*, a book of poems for which she won the Pulitzer Prize. Brooks was the first Black person to earn this prestigious writing prize. Later, Brooks taught writing at colleges and worked for the Library of Congress.

Brooks wrote some poems about brave people working for equal rights. She wrote about the lives of southern Black people, as well as life around her in the city. She said that she was like a newspaper writer, reporting the things going on around her.

10. Number the events in the order in which they happened.

    _____ Brooks wrote *Annie Allen*.

    _____ Brooks's parents set up a desk for her so that she could write.

    _____ Brooks published her first book of poems.

    _____ Brooks worked for the Library of Congress.

11. What big award did Brooks win? _____

12. Whom did Brooks write about in most of her poems? _____
    _____

13. Find an example of Gwendolyn Brooks's poetry online or at the library. What is it about? Describe the poem below.

    _____

    _____

Measurement/Writing

 Skill ID PJL

DAY 10

Convert each measurement.

1 liter (L) = 1,000 milliliters (mL)	1 gram (g) = 1,000 milligrams (mg)
1 kiloliter (kL) = 1,000 liters (L)	1 kilogram (kg) = 1,000 grams (g)

1. 1,000 mL = _____ L
2. 1,000 L = _____ kL
3. 4 L = _____ mL

4. 5 kL = _____ L
5. 8 kg = _____ g
6. 4,000 mg = _____ g

7. 9.5 g = _____ mg
8. 2 kg = _____ mg
9. 9,000 g = _____ kg

Do you think parents should limit the amount of screen time their children have? Support your opinion with reasons and evidence.

_____
_____
_____
_____
_____
_____
_____
_____
_____

Fast Fun Fact

Tornadoes have been known to move faster than Formula 1 racing cars!

Write a topic sentence for each paragraph. Try to make each topic sentence interesting so that others will want to read the paragraph.

10. They are among the world's oldest and largest living things. Some are thousands of years old and more than 200 feet (61 m) tall. Some are 100 feet (30.5 m) around at the base. They are the giant sequoia and redwood trees of California and Oregon.

_____

11. It can be a great work, like a Michelangelo carving or an African mask. It can be very large, like the Statue of Liberty, or small enough to place on a table and hold in your hand. It has always played an important part in the history of humanity. Sculpture is an excellent way to express your ideas and feelings.

_____

The rock cycle illustrates three types of changes in rocks. Write the correct phrase from the word bank on each numbered arrow. Each phrase will be used twice.

| heating and pressure | melting and crystallization | sedimentation and compaction |

12. _____
13. _____
14. _____
15. _____
16. _____
17. _____

metamorphic rock (marble)

igneous rock (basalt)

sedimentary rock (sandstone)

Percentages/Punctuation

 Skill ID **ZDZ**

DAY 11

Percentage is the comparison of a number to **100**. Write each ratio as a percentage.

1. $\frac{20}{100}$ = _____
2. $\frac{50}{100}$ = _____
3. 8:100 = _____
4. 47 to 100 = _____

Write each percentage as a fraction.

5. 19% = _____
6. 24% = _____
7. 87% = _____
8. 36% = _____

Write each percentage as a fraction. Simplify each fraction.

9. 50% = _____
10. 90% = _____
11. 20% = _____
12. 45% = _____

Sometimes, sentences include additional, nonessential pieces of information about a topic. These nonrestrictive elements should be enclosed by commas, parentheses, or dashes. Rewrite each sentence, including the nonrestrictive element shown below.

13. This year, on my nana's birthday, we will have a family picnic.
    (June 14th)

    _____

    _____

14. Jones hit the ball and the crowd went wild.
    —way into left field—

    _____

    _____

15. The new puppy got tangled up in its leash.
    , a cocker spaniel,

    _____

    _____

Context clues help you learn what words mean. Write what the underlined word means based on the context clues in the sentence.

16. Mary feigned surprise when her friends had a birthday party for her.

    _____

17. My colleagues and I work together on many new projects.

    _____

18. Maurice looks at his watch often to make sure that he is always punctual.

    _____

19. Joseph, a philatelist, has a large collection of stamps.

    _____

20. The dog napping in the shade was hardly able to bestir itself for dinner.

    _____

The steps describe how a bill becomes a law in the United States. Number the steps in the order in which they happen.

_____ Get the president's approval.

_____ Write a bill.

_____ Get a majority vote in Congress.

_____ If the president vetoes the bill, it may become a law by a two-thirds majority vote in Congress.

Mindful Moment

Go outside and look closely at the colorful world around you. Notice things that are red, orange, yellow, green, blue, and purple.

Fractions/Vocabulary

Skill IDs: ALY • XZ2

DAY 12

Write each ratio as a fraction.

1. 5 cheetahs to 7 tigers _____
2. 20 tulips to 13 roses _____
3. 12 trumpets to 5 violins _____
4. 4 taxis to 9 buses _____
5. Jill's 23¢ to Bob's 45¢ _____
6. 10 chairs to 3 tables _____
7. 1 meter to 4 meters _____
8. 3 minutes to 25 minutes _____

Use the information in the box to write each ratio as a fraction.

9. soccer balls to footballs _____
10. baseballs to soccer balls _____
11. footballs to baseballs _____
12. baseballs to all balls _____

Circle the noun or verb in parentheses that makes the information in each sentence more specific.

13. Chimpanzees live in (regions, parts) of Africa where jungle vegetation is plentiful.
14. They (hold, grip) tree branches with their palms and long fingers.
15. These (animals, primates) climb trees easily.
16. Chimpanzees eat a variety of foods, including (termites, bugs).
17. If a chimpanzee wants to eat termites, it (pokes, puts) a twig into the center of a termite mound.
18. Then, it removes the twig and (plucks, takes) off the termites.
19. If a male chimpanzee is agitated, he might (run, charge) down a hill, (taking, ripping) off tree branches.
20. He will beat the ground as he (bounds, walks) through the grass.

Read the paragraph. Then, answer the questions.

Geologists

Geology is the branch of science that deals with Earth's materials and structure. Geologists study processes such as the movement of plates on the planet's crust, volcanic eruptions, and earthquakes. Learning about these events can help scientists predict how Earth might change in the future. Some geologists study the soil to help plants grow better. Farmers can adjust the minerals in their soil to produce bigger crops. Studying water drainage helps scientists learn how to prevent flooding. Some geologists study the makeup of the sea floor, and others research gemstones. Geologists study the movement of glaciers and the use of natural resources, such as oil and gas. Many geologists collect data in the field for weeks or months and return to the laboratory to interpret their data. Geologists can be found in almost every location on Earth.

21. What is the main idea of this paragraph?

   A. Geologists study the materials and structure of Earth.

   B. Some geologists study the soil to help plants grow better.

   C. Geologists learn about different landforms.

22. What is the author's purpose in writing this selection? Explain your answer.

   _____

   _____

23. Which processes do geologists study? _____

   _____

   _____

24. Why do geologists study soil? _____

   _____

25. What do geologists do in laboratories? _____

   _____

Data Analysis/Vocabulary

Bar graphs help you compare data at a glance. Answer the questions about the bar graph.

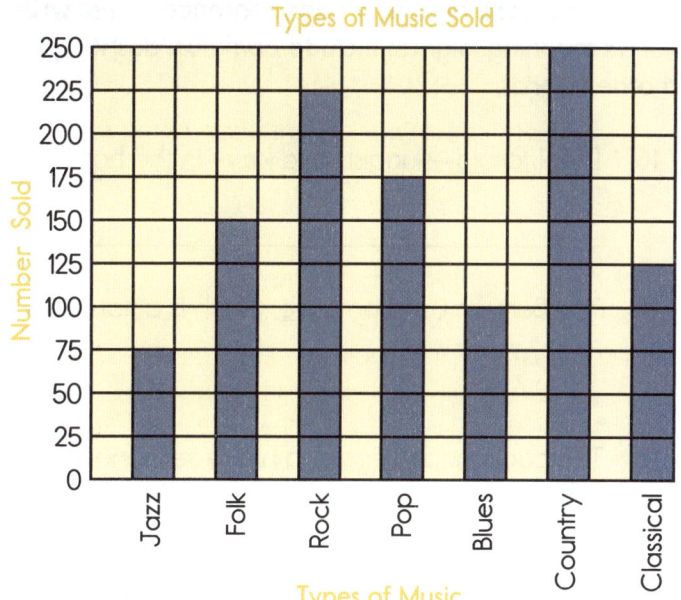

1. Which type of music was the most popular?

   _____

2. Which sold the least? _____

3. What is the difference between the greatest and the least number sold?

   _____

4. What is the average number of music sold?

   _____

5. Which is your favorite type of music?

   _____

Circle the word in parentheses that makes each sentence more descriptive.

6. The concert hall was (big, gigantic).
7. It was (ornately, nicely) decorated in red velvet and gold.
8. The (audience, people) waited eagerly for the concert to begin.
9. The (tall, towering) conductor raised his baton.
10. The (big, enormous) orchestra came to attention.
11. The audience was (very, completely) still.
12. The orchestra performed (magnificently, well).
13. The tenor sang (nicely, brilliantly).
14. The audience clapped (enthusiastically, loudly).
15. It was a (good, splendid) concert.

© Carson Dellosa Education

133

Vocabulary

Some key words and punctuation marks signal that an author is giving context clues. Write what the underlined word means in each sentence. Then, write the type of signal that helped you determine the word's meaning. Signals include commas, dashes, parentheses, and phrases such as *which is* and *in other words*.

16. I feel <u>torpid</u>—sluggish and lazy—in the hot summer weather.
    _____

17. Paul Bunyan used an <u>adze</u>, which is a flat-bladed ax, to cut down the forest.
    _____

18. The cook made <u>ragout</u>, a highly seasoned stew, every day for the ranch hands.
    _____

19. Jason bruised his <u>patella</u>, in other words, his kneecap.
    _____

20. Hakeem can play a <u>marimba</u> (a xylophone).
    _____

Affect is a verb meaning to change, influence, or act on. *Effect* is a noun meaning an impression or a result. Complete each sentence by writing *affect* or *effect* on the line.

21. The sad movie had a big _____ on Latoya.

22. The solar eclipse will _____ how bright it is outside.

23. The dog's unhealthy diet had an _____ on its energy level.

24. The high altitude will _____ our breathing.

Let's Play Today * See page 108.

Have a dance party (even if it's just you)! Turn on some of your favorite songs and dance around like no one is watching.

Data Analysis/Sentence Structure

Pie charts compare parts of a whole. Answer each question about the pie chart.

Jake earns $20 a week doing neighborhood jobs. The pie chart shows how he uses his money.

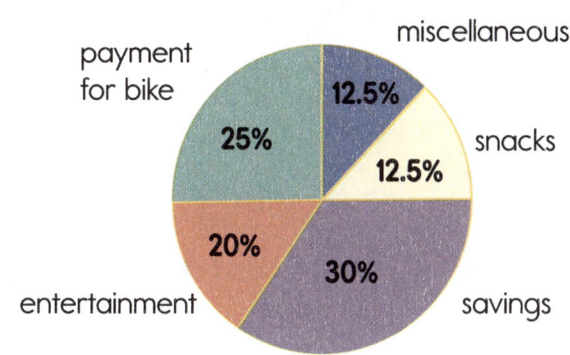

1. How much money does Jake spend on snacks each week? $ _____

2. How much does he spend on entertainment each week? $ _____

3. How much does he spend paying off his bike each week? $ _____

4. How much does he save each week? $ _____

Contractions containing *not* are called negatives. Words such as *nothing*, *nobody*, and *never* are also negatives. You should not use double negatives in writing or in speaking. Underline the double negatives in each sentence. Then, rewrite the sentence without the double negative.

5. The fight <u>didn't</u> solve <u>nothing</u>.
   The fight didn't solve anything.

6. The team didn't want no trouble.
   _____

7. Haven't you never seen Yellowstone National Park?
   _____

8. There aren't no eggs in the carton.
   _____

9. He wasn't near no base when he was tagged out.
   _____

10. There isn't no way to get there from here.
    _____

11. The explanation didn't make no sense.
    _____

Divide fractions to solve the word problems.

12. A carpenter cuts a board that is $\frac{4}{5}$ meters long into pieces that are $\frac{2}{3}$ meters long. How many pieces will he have?

13. Emil has $8\frac{1}{2}$ ounces of salsa. If he divides it into containers that hold $4\frac{1}{4}$ ounces each, how many containers can he fill?

14. Cara has $\frac{6}{9}$ yard of ribbon. She cuts the ribbon into 3 equal pieces. What is the length of each piece?

15. Adita uses a $4\frac{1}{2}$-pound bag of potting soil to fill 6 pots. How many pounds of soil will be in each pot?

Match each word with its definition. Use a dictionary, a science book, or the Internet if you need help.

16. _____ asteroids

    A. an object that orbits a planet or a moon

17. _____ comet

    B. rocky or metal objects that orbit the sun in a belt between Mars and Jupiter; also called planetoids or minor planets

18. _____ star

    C. a huge ball of glowing gas that can exist for billions of years; our sun is the closest one

19. _____ satellite

    D. a small object orbiting the sun that is made of frozen ice, gas, and dust; it has a tail that always points away from the sun

20. _____ planet

    E. a large body that orbits a star and does not produce its own light; there are eight in our solar system

Data Analysis/Sentence Structure

A pictograph uses picture symbols to represent different amounts of data or specific units. Answer each question about the pictograph.

School Visitors

Monday	🚶 🚶 🚶 🚶 🚶 🚶 🚶 🚶
Tuesday	🚶 🚶 🚶 🚶 🚶 🚶
Wednesday	🚶 🚶 🚶
Thursday	🚶 🚶 🚶
Friday	🚶 🚶 🚶 🚶 🚶 🚶

🚶 = 10 family members

This pictograph shows how many family members visited Riverton School during Family Week.

1. When did most family members visit? _____

2. What does 🚶 stand for? _____

3. How many family members visited the school during Family Week? _____

4. When did the least number of family members visit? _____

5. How many family members visited on Friday? _____

6. What other type of graph could have been used to show this data? _____

Underline the double negatives in each sentence. Then, rewrite the sentence correctly.

7. Can't no one solve the puzzle? _____
_____

8. Rick didn't have nothing to read. _____
_____

9. There isn't nothing you can do about it. _____
_____

David Glasgow Farragut

Read the passage. Then, answer the questions.

At age nine, David Glasgow Farragut went to sea. Farragut's father, who was Spanish, came to the United States in 1776. He fought for his new country in the American Revolution and the War of 1812. Farragut's mother died when he was seven, so he was sent to live with naval captain David Porter. Porter found a place on a ship for Farragut.

Farragut was at sea during the War of 1812. When he was 12 years old, he was put in charge of a prize ship that had been captured from the enemy. Farragut's job was to get the ship safely to port. This was a hard job during a war, but Farragut did it.

After many years of peace, a war about slavery broke out—the Civil War. Farragut loved his home in Virginia, but he told his wife that he was "sticking to the flag." So, the couple moved to New York. David Farragut was 60 years old.

The Mississippi River was guarded too well for the North to use it. Farragut was asked to **capture** New Orleans, Louisiana. It was an important port for the Confederacy and the gateway to the huge river system. Farragut took his flagship, the *Hartford*, and almost 50 other ships with him. He captured New Orleans and other cities on the Mississippi. Finally, in 1864, he turned to Mobile, Alabama. Under heavy fire, Farragut captured Mobile, the Confederacy's last big port.

In less than two years, the *Hartford* had been hit 240 times by cannon fire. The war was almost over. Farragut went home to New York. He was made an admiral for the important work he did during the Civil War.

10. What does the word *capture* mean in the passage?

    A. to take control of   **B.** to guard   **C.** to keep safe   **D.** to clothe

11. Number the events in the order in which they happened.

    _____ Farragut brought a captured ship safely to port.
    _____ Farragut captured the port of Mobile, Alabama.
    _____ Farragut was sent to live with a navy captain.
    _____ Farragut fought battles on the Mississippi River.

12. What city did Farragut have to capture to get to the Mississippi River? _____

13. What rank was Farragut given at the end of the war? _____

Fast Fun Fact

Frogs rained down in Serbia after a tornado sucked up water and its inhabitants and then dumped them out as it traveled along land.

Geometry/Capitalization, Punctuation, & Spelling

Follow the instructions and answer the question.

1. Plot Point A at (−6, 4).

2. Point B is at the same distance above the x-axis as Point A, but it is 10 units away on the opposite side of the y-axis. Plot Point B and write its coordinates: (____, ____).

3. Draw a line connecting A and B.

4. Plot Point C at (8, −4) and draw a line connecting B and C.

5. Point D is at the same distance below the x-axis as Point C, but it is 17 units away on the opposite side of the y-axis. Plot Point D and write its coordinates: (____, ____).

6. Draw a line connecting C and D.

7. Draw a line connecting D and A.

8. What shape have you drawn on the coordinate plane? _____

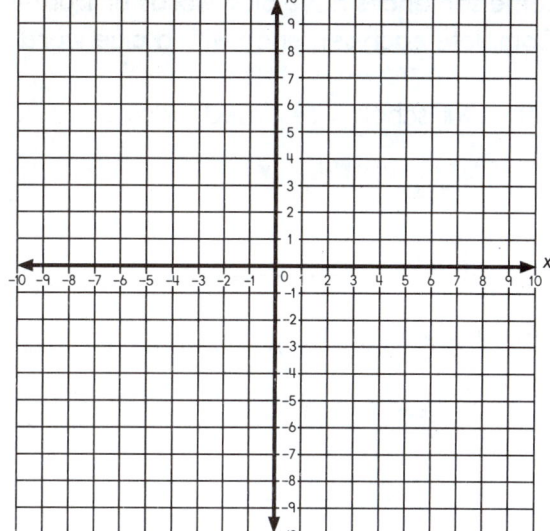

Correct the paragraph. Draw three lines under each letter that needs to be capitalized. Cross out each misspelled word and write the correct spelling above the word. Add punctuation where needed.

jokingly named the "Highest Court in the Land," the basketbal court and gym on the fith floor of the united states supreme court building was bilt in the 1940s it is located in wat used to be a large storage area No one realy knows why the storage area was converted into a gym and basketball court, but it gets used by cafateria workers, security gards, librarians, law clerks, and even justises who precide over the oficial Highest Court of the Land It is rumored that supreme court Justices brett kavanaugh and elena kagan have shot sum hoops up here!

Some sentences have clue words or transition words that help show cause-and-effect relationships. Complete each sentence with a clue word or transition word. Then, write the cause and effect.

9. Our school was closed today <u>because</u> of the snowstorm we had last night.

   Cause: <u>snowstorm</u>

   Effect: <u>school was closed</u>

10. It snowed all day, _____ the ground was white.

    Cause: _____

    Effect: _____

11. Our electricity went out last night, _____ we went out to dinner.

    Cause: _____

    Effect: _____

12. Joe left the gate unlatched, _____ all of the cattle were out in the road.

    Cause: _____

    Effect: _____

Pollution is a problem that affects all living things on Earth. Match each term with its description.

13. _____ leaked oil from a tanker that ran aground   A. greenhouse effect

14. _____ poisonous materials such as paint thinner   B. hazardous waste

15. _____ smoke and exhaust that mix with water vapor   C. acid rain

16. _____ a warming of the surface and lower atmosphere of Earth   D. oil spill

Mindful Moment

Finish this sentence, and then draw a picture to go with it:
"I am grateful for . . ."

Numbers/Sentence Structure

Write the integer for each letter on the number line.

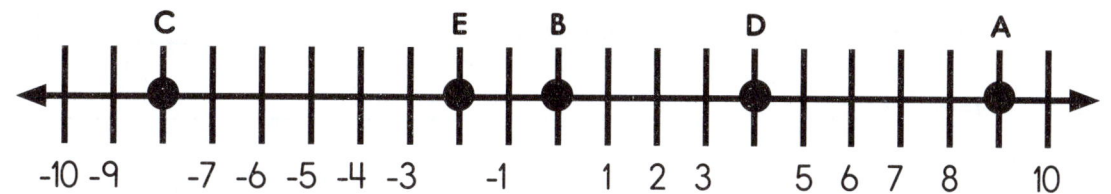

1. A = ____
2. B = ____
3. C = ____
4. D = ____
5. E = ____

Write >, <, or = to compare each pair of numbers.

6. -8 ◯ 8
7. 0 ◯ -3
8. 15 ◯ -16
9. -4 ◯ 4
10. -12 ◯ -20
11. -3 ◯ -4

Use the common predicates or subjects in each group of sentences to write a single sentence.

12. Jim liked to visit Grandma and Grandpa. Sean liked to visit Grandma and Grandpa. Maria liked to visit Grandma and Grandpa.

   _____

   _____

13. Grandma raised chickens. Grandma raised ducks. Grandma raised geese.

   _____

   _____

14. Daisies grew in her garden. Tulips grew in her garden. Roses grew in her garden.

   _____

   _____

Day 17

Language Arts

Write an effect to complete each sentence. Look for clue words or transition words.

15. The old house had not been painted in years, so <u>the first thing we did was paint it</u>.

16. The oven temperature was too high, so _____.

17. _____ because my new shoes were too tight.

18. The wind was blowing hard, so _____.

19. Because I didn't get up early enough this morning, _____.

Write a cause to complete each sentence.

20. The plane was delayed due to _____.

21. _____, so my stomach hurt.

22. _____, so we decided to celebrate.

23. The drinks were very sweet because _____.

Add commas where they are needed in these sentences that list a series of items.

24. Of tennis baseball hockey and karate, I like karate the best.

25. I have tried playing the flute saxophone drums violin and tuba.

26. The storm brought hail sleet and rain to our town.

27. We had to take a train bus taxi and shuttle to get to our destination.

Data Analysis/Parts of Speech

Use the Venn diagram to compare each set of data.

1. Mark, Heather, and Charita compared the multiples of 4 and 5.
   Multiples of 4: 0, 4, 8, 12, 16, 20
   Multiples of 5: 0, 5, 10, 15, 20, 25

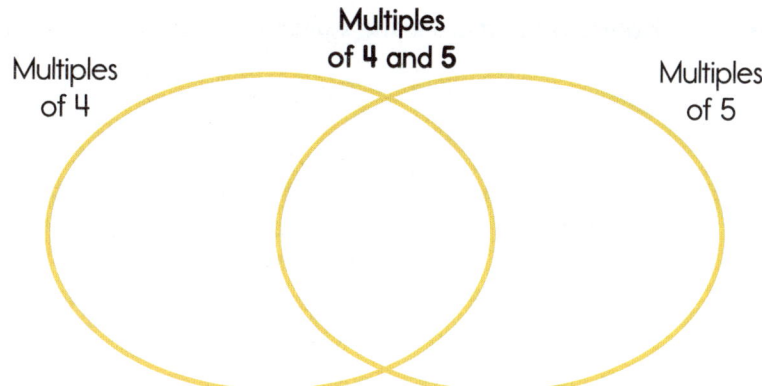

2. Cameron, Sean, and Alexandra compared the diameters of the seeds they found.
   Cameron: 0.5 cm, 1 cm, 1.5 cm, 2 cm
   Sean: 0.5 cm, 1.5 cm, 3 cm, 3.5 cm
   Alexandra: 0.25 cm, 0.5 cm, 2 cm, 3 cm

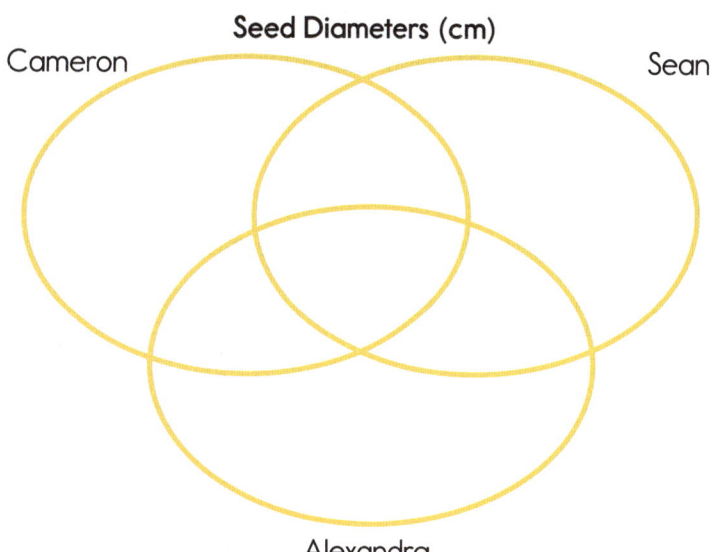

Circle the possessive pronoun that correctly completes each sentence.

3. Mariana collects books, and she likes (**her**, she) old books best.
4. Ty said that (he, his) parents also collect books.
5. Emily washed (her, hers) hair.
6. I asked (my, mine) sister to give me a ride home.
7. The cat bathed (hers, her) kittens.
8. The girls made lunch for (their, theirs) family.

Reading Comprehension

Read the poem. Then, answer the questions.

"The Road Not Taken" by Robert Frost

Two roads diverged in a yellow wood,
And sorry I could not travel both
And be one traveler, long I stood
And looked down one as far as I could
To where it bent in the undergrowth;
Then took the other, as just as fair,
And having perhaps the better claim,
Because it was grassy and wanted wear;
Though as for that the passing there
Had worn them really about the same,

And both that morning equally lay
In leaves no step had trodden black.
Oh, I kept the first for another day!
Yet knowing how way leads on to way,
I doubted if I should ever come back.
I shall be telling this with a sigh
Somewhere ages and ages hence:
Two roads diverged in a wood, and I—
I took the one less traveled by,
And that has made all the difference.

9. After you read the poem, visit www.poets.org/poem/road-not-taken to listen to Robert Frost reading it himself. How is your experience listening to the poet read the poem different than reading it yourself? Use a separate sheet of paper if necessary for your answer.

_____

_____

10. What is the main idea of this poem?

_____

_____

11. Reread the last stanza of the poem. How does it bring the poem to a conclusion?

_____

_____

 **Let's Play Today** * See page 108.

Pretend that you are chopping vegetables with your hands in the air in front of you. Do this for one minute.

Geometry/Grammar

DAY 19

Follow the directions for the coordinate graph.

1. Plot each coordinate pair and label each point.

   (2, 2) A   (12, 8) L
   (12, 16) H   (8, 10) D
   (16, 12) J   (10, 8) N
   (6, 4) P   (13, 13) I
   (14, 10) K   (6, 8) C
   (10, 14) G   (10, 11) E
   (4, 6) B   (11, 10) M
   (8, 12) F
   (8, 6) O

2. Connect points A through P in alphabetical order.

3. Connect point P to point A.

4. Connect point E to point I and point I to point M.

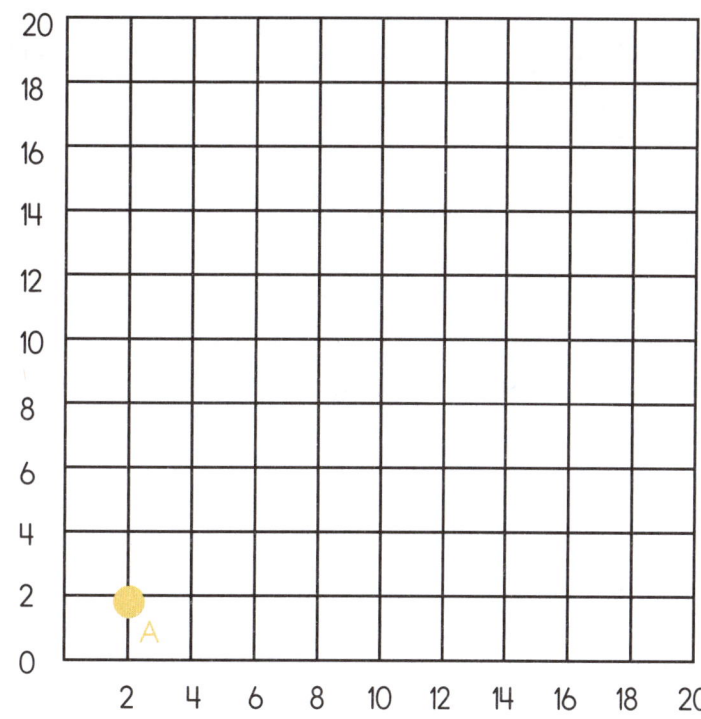

The pronouns *who* and *whom* can be used to ask a question or introduce a clause. *Who* is used when the pronoun is the subject. *Whom* is used when the pronoun is an object. Write *who* or *whom* to complete each sentence.

5. _____ made the first moon landing?

6. _____ do you like the best among the candidates?

7. _____ is your best friend?

8. _____ won the gold medal?

9. _____ does Ryan think will be the best choice for the math contest?

10. _____ was the man she saw walking his dog?

11. _____ shall I call in case of an emergency?

12. He is the person _____ is always late!

DAY 19

Language Arts/Writing

Underline the noun that is being personified in each sentence. Then, write the personifying word or words.

13. The first-place trophy proudly stood on the shelf in Damien's room.

    _____

14. Because we could not go out to play, we watched from our window as the clouds spit sleet.

    _____

15. Autumn leaves seemed to sing as they danced across the lawn.

    _____

16. Horns honked angrily as drivers became impatient.

    _____

17. The sun played hide-and-seek with me as it popped in and out of the clouds.

    _____

Because of women like Lucy Stone, Susan B. Anthony, Septima Poinsette Clark, Elizabeth Cady Stanton, and Dr. Mabel Ping-Hua Lee, women in the United States have many rights today that they didn't have in earlier times. Research one of these women and write a paragraph about the trials she had to go through because of what she believed.

_____

_____

_____

_____

_____

_____

Data Analysis/Grammar

Box plots are used to determine the distribution of data. Look at the example below. The results of a test might include these 15 scores: 48, 56, 65, 66, 72, 73, 74, 75, 77, 81, 83, 85, 87, 89, 98. Make sure the data is arranged in numerical order. Then, plot the median (75) on a number line. The lower quartile is the median of the lower half (66). The upper quartile is the median of the upper half (85). Draw a box around the median with its ends going through the quartiles. Each quartile contains one-fourth of the scores. Some people call this type of graph a box-and-whisker plot. The "whiskers" are the two lines extending to the highest and lowest values of the data.

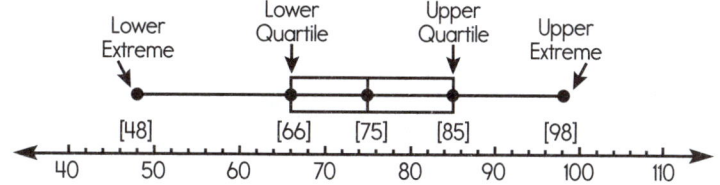

1. Using the number line below, draw a box plot for these scores: 10, 15, 15, 20, 20, 25, 30, 30, 35, 40, 40.

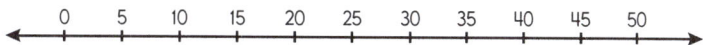

2. What is the median score? _____

3. What is the lower quartile? _____

4. What is the upper quartile? _____

The verb *can* is used to express mental or physical ability. *May* is used to express possibility or ask permission. The verb *lie* means to rest or recline. The verb *lay* means to put or place something. Circle the verb that correctly completes each sentence.

5. Bingo, (lie, lay) down!

6. Toto (may, can) do several tricks, such as sitting, shaking, and rolling over.

7. Mom, (may, can) Amy spend the night on Friday?

8. Please (lie, lay) the paper on the stairs.

DAY 20

Language Arts/Science

Circle the mood of each sentence.

9. The grayish clouds overshadowed the day.
   A. happy
   B. sad
   C. quiet

10. Larry looked toward the ground and tried to hold back his tears.
    A. happy
    B. sad
    C. quiet

11. As the waves slowly touched the shore, the water whispered softly.
    A. happy
    B. sad
    C. quiet

12. The clown's bright costume jiggled as he played with the perky puppy.
    A. happy
    B. sad
    C. quiet

13. The children's laughter floated through the air as they splashed in the pool.
    A. happy
    B. sad
    C. quiet

14. A hushed silence fell over the crowd.
    A. happy
    B. sad
    C. quiet

Match each inventor with their invention. Use the Internet if you need help.

15. _____ Eli Whitney
16. _____ Madam C. J. Walker
17. _____ Levi Strauss
18. _____ Virginia Apgar
19. _____ Samuel F. B. Morse
20. _____ Thomas Edison
21. _____ Stephanie Kwolek

A. telegraph
B. phonograph
C. hair care products
D. cotton gin
E. Kevlar
F. health test for newborns
G. blue jeans

Fast Fun Fact

A cloud can weigh over one million pounds!

Science Experiment

How Do Lungs Work?*

Have you ever wondered how your lungs are able to breathe in and out? In this activity, you will learn about how lungs work.

Materials
- balloons (2 small, 1 large)
- 2-liter plastic bottle
- masking tape
- rubber bands (small and large)
- 2 pipettes
- rubber tubing
- scissors

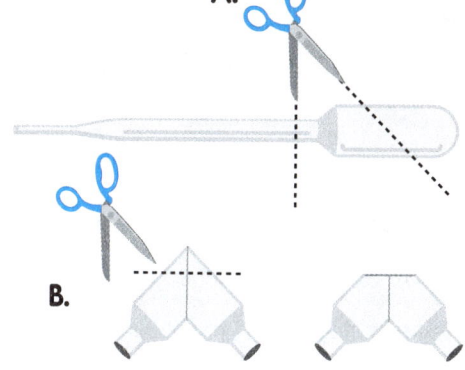

Procedure
1. Cut the pipettes (A). You may need an adult's help.
2. Place the pipette bulbs together and hold them together with tape. Then, cut off the tops of the bulbs, creating a "Y" connector (B).
3. Insert your new Y-shaped piece into the rubber tubing and tape it in place. Attach the two small balloons to the arms of the "Y" with small rubber bands.
4. Have an adult help you cut off the bottom of the 2-liter bottle.
5. Insert the tubing through the bottom of the bottle and out through the neck. Use tape to seal the tubing at the neck so that the balloons are suspended inside the bottle.
6. Cut the neck off the large balloon. Stretch the rest of the balloon over the bottom of the bottle. Use a large rubber band to keep it in place.
7. Pull on the bottom of the balloon, being careful not to pull it off the bottle. Watch what happens to the small balloons.

What's This All About?
The long tube at the top represents your trachea, where the air comes in. The two arms of the plastic piece represent bronchial tubes, which lead to the lungs. The small balloons are the lungs. By pulling on the bottom balloon, which represents the diaphragm (a large muscle under the lungs), you lower the pressure inside the bottle (your chest cavity). This causes the "lungs" to inflate because the outside air pressure is now higher than the inside air pressure and air rushes in to equalize it. When you let go of the diaphragm, you increase the inside air pressure and the lungs deflate as the air rushes out. The diaphragm (with help from other muscles) pulls air into the lungs and pushes it out again. While the air is inside, the lungs collect carbon dioxide from the blood and put oxygen back into it. The carbon dioxide is then pushed out with the next exhale.

* See page 2.

Science Experiment

Building Bridges

Which shape will support the most weight? Build these bridges to find out.

Materials
- paper
- scissors
- tape
- toy cars

Procedure

1. Fold a piece of paper lengthwise three times to create a square tube. Make sure the folds are the same distance apart so it is square, not rectangular. Tape the ends together to close the tube.
2. Repeat step 1 with three lengthwise folds to create a triangular tube. Make a second triangular tube.
3. Use scissors to cut each tube into sections that are 1.5-2 inches wide. You should end up with about 7 shallow square tubes and about 14 shallow triangular tubes.
4. Cut two strips of paper that are about 11" x 2" (28 cm x 3 cm). This will be your road surface. You may need to tape the ends of strips together to create longer roads.
5. Place the square tubes side by side with the left and right sides touching (see diagram A). Place the paper road on top to create a bridge.

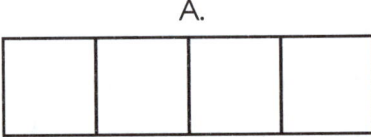
A.

6. Place two triangle tubes side by side so their bottom corners touch. Then, place a triangle point-down between them (see diagram B). Repeat until at least 11 triangles have been used. Place the paper road on top to create a bridge.

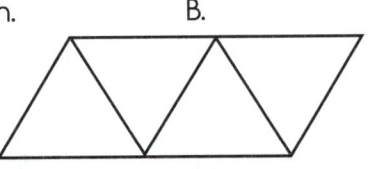
B.

7. Drive a toy car across each bridge. What happens? Next, try heavier and lighter cars, or add more than one car.
8. Repeat steps 1-7 with different folds to test the strength of different shapes, such as circles, rectangles, or pentagons.

What's This All About?
Square bridge supports can't hold the weight of a car. That is because the top of the square holds all of the force and the sides bow out. Triangles can hold more weight because, when weight presses down on the top point, the force is evenly divided down each side and shared equally by the base.

© Carson Dellosa Education

Social Studies Activity

Governing a Nation

The United States Constitution is organized into seven sections called *articles*. The articles are numbered with Roman numerals. Match each article with its summary. Use an encyclopedia, the Internet, or another reference if you need help.

1. _____ Article I
2. _____ Article II
3. _____ Article III
4. _____ Article IV
5. _____ Article V
6. _____ Article VI
7. _____ Article VII

A. says that at least nine states must accept the Constitution before it can become a law

B. states that the Constitution is the law of the land and that all senators and representatives must swear to support the Constitution

C. describes the powers of the Supreme Court and other federal courts

D. describes how the president will be elected, who can run for president, and what powers and responsibilities the president has

E. describes how the states will relate to each other, how new states can be added to the Union, and how the federal government will protect the states

F. describes how amendments, or changes, can be made to the Constitution

G. describes how Congress will be set up, how laws will be made, and what powers Congress will have

Read each description of Canada's system of government. Then, fill in the blanks to complete each description of the U.S. government.

8. Canada is comprised of 10 provinces and three territories. The United States is comprised of _____ states, the _____ of Columbia, and territories.

9. Canada is a parliamentary democracy and a constitutional monarchy, with a king or queen of England as its head of state. The United States is a constitutional _____ with a _____ as its head of state.

10. Each province in Canada has its own legislature and is governed by a federally appointed commissioner. Each U.S. state has its own _____ and is governed by a _____ .

United States Supreme Court

Read the paragraph. Then, write *yes* or *no* to answer each question.

The U.S. Supreme Court is the highest court in the country. Its main job is to rule on cases that involve questions about laws in the Constitution. The Supreme Court also has the last say in cases that have gone through the lower courts. The Supreme Court is not like a trial court. Instead of one judge, there are nine, and there is no jury of U.S. citizens to make the decisions. The judges make the final decisions, called *rulings*. The Supreme Court cannot make new laws, but their rulings are similar to laws because all other courts must follow their decisions. The judges on the U.S. Supreme Court are called *justices*. Supreme Court justices are chosen by the president of the United States with approval from the Senate. After a judge is chosen as a Supreme Court justice, he or she has the job for life.

1. Can another court change the decision of a Supreme Court ruling? _____

2. Does the Supreme Court use a jury to make decisions? _____

3. Do other courts have to follow Supreme Court rulings? _____

4. Is there more than one judge on the Supreme Court? _____

5. Does the U.S. Senate choose the Supreme Court justices? _____

6. Does a Supreme Court justice lose his or her job after 10 years? _____

7. Can the Supreme Court write new laws? _____

8. Does the Supreme Court settle questions about the Constitution? _____

Look up the current Supreme Court justices and write their names below.

_____   _____

_____   _____

_____   _____

_____   _____

Social Studies Activity

The States

Read the paragraph. Then, circle *true* or *false* for each statement.

Each state in the United States has such different concerns that federal laws cannot meet each state's specific needs. State government allows each state to make rules and laws that are specific to its state. Each state has a capital city where the government does its work. The organization of state government is similar to the organization of the federal government. Each state in the United States has an executive, a legislative, and a judicial branch of government. The executive branch in state government is headed by the state's governor. The legislative branch in all state governments except Nebraska has an upper house (usually called a *senate*) and a lower house (usually called a *house of representatives*) to make laws. (Nebraska has just one state house.) The judicial branch in state government contains state courts and a state supreme court. Each state also has its own constitution. One state's constitution and laws can be very different from another's but cannot go against the U.S. Constitution.

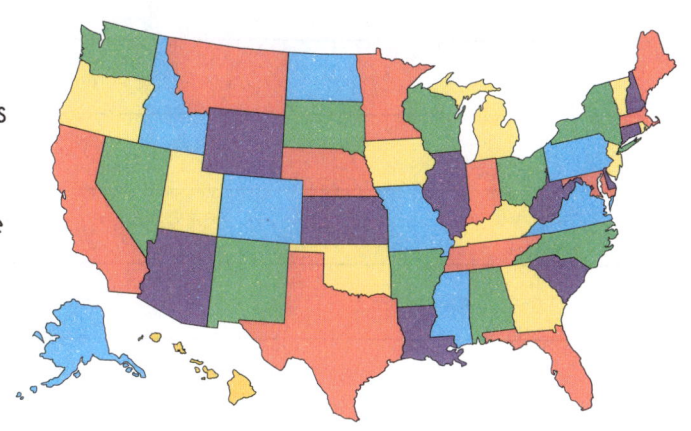

1. Each state's constitution is the same.   true   false
2. Each state has three branches of government.   true   false
3. Every state has two houses in the legislative branch.   true   false
4. Every state has a governor.   true   false
5. A state's constitution can keep women from voting in that state.   true   false
6. A governor is to a state as the president is to the country.   true   false
7. State governments do their work in Washington, D.C.   true   false
8. Federal laws are not specific enough to meet all states' needs.   true   false
9. Each state has a supreme court.   true   false
10. The executive branch makes the laws in state government.   true   false

© Carson Dellosa Education

Reflect and Reset

Think back on your year of fifth grade. What was the hardest part?

_____
_____
_____
_____
_____

What was your favorite part of fifth grade?

_____
_____
_____
_____
_____

Look ahead to this coming year of sixth grade. What might be a challenge?

_____
_____
_____
_____
_____

Answer Key

Section 1

Day 1/Page 13:
1. 21,411; 2. 84,525; 3. 892; 4. 519,549; 5. 1,212; 6. 66 R 6; 7. 42,094; 8. $1,668.41; 9. B; 10. A; 11. B; 12. A; 13. - 22. Answers will vary. 23. 120; 24. 15; 25. 23; 26. 72; 27. 6; 28. 4; 29. 65; 30. 300; 31. 128; 32. 50

Day 2/Page 15:
1. 2,685,322; 2. 478.53; 3. 23,409,036; 4. 2,111.097; 5. (3 × 10,000,000) + (7 × 1,000,000) + (1 × 100,000) + (2 × 10,000) + (6 × 1,000) + (4 × 100) + (8 × 10) + (9 × 1) + (2 × $\frac{1}{10}$); 6. (2 × 1,000) + (6 × 10) + (9 × 1) + (4 × $\frac{1}{100}$) + (4 × $\frac{1}{1000}$); 7. for; 8. about; 9. on; 10. into; 11. to; 12. beyond; 13. after; 14. in; 15. camping; 16. packed; 17. hunt; 18. picked; 19. Parking; 20. splashing; 21. Anchorage; 22. Los Angeles; 23. Kansas City; 24. New Orleans; 25. Detroit; 26. Ottawa; 27. Albuquerque; 28. New York City; 29. Columbus; 30. Calgary

Day 3/Page 17:
works work, goes go, likes like, chooses choose, has have, finishes finish, shares share, meets meet, enjoys enjoy; 1. spice, Variety makes life interesting.; 2. cake, You can't have everything you want.; 3. basket, Don't count on any one thing.; 4. leap, Think about what you are going to do before you do it.; 5. turn, When you do something kind for someone, they will return the favor.; 6. The Lunar Module had landed on the moon.; 7. moon; 8. because the astronauts might not get another chance to go to the moon or to return to *Apollo 11*; 9. They were the first people to walk on the moon.; 10. Answers will vary.

Day 4/Page 19:
1. A, C, E, F, H, I; 2. E, J; 3. A, B; 4. E, F, H; 5. A, G; 6. D, E; 7. B; 8. C, E, F; 9. geography; 10. transportation; 11. extract; 12. meteorology; 13.-24. Answers will vary.; Students' writing will vary.

Day 5/Page 21:
1. 5; 2. 9; 3. 4; 4. 6; 5. 2; 6. 8; 7. both, and; 8. Just as, so; 9. Neither, nor; 10. either, or; 11. not only, but; 12. Neither, nor; 13. Either, or; 14. Whether, or; 15. the act of punishing; 16. vanish; 17. to soak before; 18. to wind again; 19. without color; 20. cooked before; 21. not sure; 22. like brown; 23. The vibration of the loud music made the car thump.; 24. If you want an honest opinion, ask someone you can trust.; 25. Some students grasped the concept, while others were confused.; 26. A large glacier broke apart as the sea became rough.

Day 6/Page 23:
1. $7\frac{5}{8}$; 2. $4\frac{1}{12}$; 3. $3\frac{4}{21}$; 4. $1\frac{1}{2}$; 5. $1\frac{1}{3}$; 6. $7\frac{1}{2}$; 7. 96; 8. $\frac{1}{36}$; 9. - 12. Answers will vary; 13. C; 14. an ecosystem; 15. Answers may include: grasslands, wetlands, tundra, mountain, maritime, temperate rainforests, temperate deciduous forests. 16. permafrost 17. It is near the Atlantic Ocean.; 18. the Hudson Plains; 19. the sea

Day 7/Page 25:
1. 28.875; 2. 661; 3. 123.773; 4. 98.5; 5. 9; 6. 184.6; 7. 99.333; 8. 83.2; Book reviews will vary.; 9. G; 10. C; 11. H; 12. B; 13. D; 14. F; 15. E; 16. A; 17. 45 years; 18. 27 years; 19. 18 years; 20. 48 years

Day 8/Page 27:
1. $1\frac{7}{15}$ pounds; 2. $6\frac{13}{84}$ feet tall; 3. $2\frac{17}{60}$ hours; 4. $1\frac{7}{40}$ hours; Circled action verbs include: walk, sound, call, dance, wore, gather, sneezed, read, eat, cheer, cry, built, speak, blew, clapping, watched, chews; Underlined linking verbs include: are, be, seem, being, will, were, is, am, become, have been, was, became, have; 5. stethoscope; 6. suspicious; 7. margin; 8. owes; 9. knead; 10. allergies; 11. conduct; 12. inlets; Solids: dust, rock, ice, box; Liquids: juice, lava, milk, water; Gases: air, helium, oxygen, hydrogen

Day 9/Page 29:
1. 0.7; 2. 160; 3. 25; 4. 4,200; 5. 4,500; 6. 4.2; 7. 12,000; 8. 2,700; 9. 150,000; 10. am; 11. is; 12. were; 13. was; 14. Are; 15. has been; 16. is being; 17. will be; 18. – 20. Answers will vary.; 21. North Carolina; 22. four years; 23. Answers will vary. ; 24. Answers will vary.

Day 10/Page 31:
1. 38,822; 2. 16,936; 3. 15,687; 4. 49,623; 5. 172,072; 6. 288,357; 7. 90,741; 8. 457,666; 9. wore; 10. rang; 11. chose; 12. spent; 13. awoke; 14. became; 15. brought; 16. drew; 17. grew; 18. Ok,; 19. Shh!; 20. Ouch,; 21. Wow!; 22. Hmmm,; 23. Really,; 24. Stop!; 25. hold on,; 26. from the patio; 27. For thirty minutes; 28. with a lot of emotion; 29. Without listening to directions; 30. Behind the refrigerator

Day 11/Page 33:
1. 42; 2. 72; 3. 25; 4. 55; 5. 24; 6. 54; 7. 0; 8. 54; 9. 50; 10. 110; 11. 27; 12. 108; 13. 36; 14. 90; 15. 28; 16. 48; 17. 56; 18. 99; 19. 48; 20. 70; 21. 132; 22. 21; 23. 81; 24. 55; 25. 35; 26. 120; 27. 63; 28. 100; 29. 22; 30. 72; 31. 40; 32. 66; 33. held; 34. bled; 35. wrote; 36. rode; 37. taught; 38. froze; 39. (84 ÷ 12) + 16; 40. (12 × 7) - 14; 41. (63 ÷ 9) × 7; 42. (54 - 32) × (8 - 5); 43. (36 ÷ 3) × (15 - 2); 44. removed; 45. cash crops; 46. indigo; 47. plantations

Day 12/Page 35:
1. 125 cm³; 2. 8 ft.³; 3. 343 yd.³; 4. 1,000 mm³; 5. 1,728 in.³; 6. 1 m³; 7. tear, swim, ring, sing, see, begin, eat, go; 8. tore, swam, rang, sang, saw, began, ate, went; 9. has/have torn, swum, rung, sung, seen, begun, eaten, gone; 10. remodel; 11. deposit; 12. giggle; 13. shelves; 14. penalty; 15. predict; 16. precise; 17. estimate; 18. business; 19. giant; Students' writing will vary.

Day 13/Page 37:

Point	x	y	(x, y)
A	1	3	(1, 3)
B	2	4	(2, 4)
C	3	5	(3, 5)
D	4	6	(4, 6)
E	5	7	(5, 7)
F	6	8	(6, 8)
G	7	9	(7, 9)

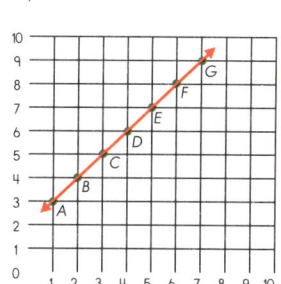

1. will build; 2. will check; 3. will map; 4. will board; 5. will count; 6. will launch; 7. will view; 8. will observe; 9. 4; 10. Precambrian, Paleozoic, Mesozoic, Cenozoic; 11. Mesozoic; 12. 3; 13. Triassic, Jurassic, Cretaceous; 14. Cenozoic

Day 14/Page 39:
1. jumbo; 2. 6 dozen small eggs; 3. large; 4. 72, small; 5. 120 ounces;

Answer Key

6. Stargirl; 7. The Wizard of Oz; 8. Walk Two Moons, Wonder; 9. Grease, "Summer Nights"; 10. Peter Pan; 11. "The Wheels on the Bus"; 12. Star Wars; 13. Fresh Off the Boat; Febuary February, Journel Journal, definatley definitely, calender calendar, naybor neighbor, suprised surprised, cuboards cupboards, vacume vacuum, your you're, especialy especially, priviledge privilege, untill until; 1.–5. Questions will vary.

Day 15/Page 41:
1. $249\frac{1}{2}$; 2. 644 ml; 3. $64\frac{2}{5}$; 4. 56 ml; 5. Answers will vary but could include asparagas.; 6. between *dilute* and *julienne*; 7. julienne; 8. a pot roast; 9. – 16. Answers will vary.; 17. plane; 18. flower; 19. throne; 20. scent; 21. toe; 22. blew

Day 16/Page 43:
1. use; 2. propels; 3. are; 4. enjoy; 5. steers; 6. is; Students should circle the words in bold: 7. **wild**, **eerie**, wind; 8. **fuzzy**, **brown**, caterpillar; 9. **fresh**, **cool**, water; 10. **hot**, **tired**, explorers; **large**, **clear**, lake 11. longest; 12. wider; 13. youngest; 14. largest; 15. smaller; 16. seeping into, filling; 17. *he scraped and scratched and scrabbled and scrooged and then he scrooged again and scrabbled and scratched and scraped*, Answers will vary. Possible answer: The repeated sounds of the words are similar to the mole's motions as he digs. Alliteration makes the description more interesting to read. 18. Answers will vary. Possible answer: Grahame shows how busy the mole is and how hard he is working. Grahame also shows the reader that even though the mole is industrious, he is willing to give up his cleaning to enjoy the spring day.

Day 17/Page 45:
1. $2\frac{1}{8}$ hours; 2. $2\frac{8}{15}$ pounds; 3. $2\frac{7}{12}$ cups; 4. $8\frac{5}{24}$ miles; 5. PN; 6. PA; 7. PN; 8. PA; 9. PA; 10. PN; 11. PA; 12. PA; **Across:** 2. smart, 3. great, 4. chew, 5. remember, 6. doctor; **Down:** 1. wellknown (well-known), 2. starving, 3. grabbed, 4. crowd; 2, 1, 5, 6, 7, 4, 3

Day 18/Page 47:
1. $2\frac{3}{8}$ cups of dry pasta; 2. $19\frac{1}{4}$ inches; 3. 40 napkins; 4. 18 cups of tea; 5. immediately, lately, never, often, soon, today; 6. carefully, eagerly, hard, quickly, softly, wildly; 7. above, far, here, inside, there, upstairs; 8. moist; 9. enclosed; 10. ignorant; 11. outer core, inner core; 12. mantle; 13. lithosphere; 14. core; 15. center of Earth

Day 19/Page 49:
1. $1\frac{7}{8}$; 2. $1\frac{5}{42}$; 3. $2\frac{11}{14}$; 4. $1\frac{11}{12}$; 5. $3\frac{5}{6}$; 6. $3\frac{3}{8}$; 7. <; 8. =; 9. >; 10. <; 11. =; 12. =; 13. had explained; 14. had tried; 15. has visited; 16. will have returned; 17. has been excited; 18. will have played; 19. had hoped; 20. will have read; 21. A; 22. Answers may include: Olympic Games, democracy, statues, buildings, medical texts, trade routes, epic poetry; 23. Modern sports arenas are based on ancient Greek stadiums; 24. The author explains facts about Greek contributions to medicine, trade routes, and poetry; 25. Their medical texts were used for hundreds of years.

Day 20/Page 51:
1. 6; 2. 10; 3. 5; 4. 16; 5. 48; 6. 12; 7. 15; 8. 21; 9. 48; 10. 15; 11. 60; 12. 9; 13. Meanwhile, Mom and Dad wrapped Diego's gift.; 14. After the storm had blown over, Grandpa went outside to survey the damage.; 15. You haven't locked your keys in the car, have you?; 16. Yes, I think the outfit you're wearing is appropriate for the recital.; 17. Furthermore, you didn't do any of your chores this week.; 18. Did you remember to lock the back door, Danny?; 19. Next, mix the milk, oil, and egg into the dry ingredients.; 20. Dr. Alonzo, have you received the results of the tests yet?; 21. enjoys; 22. destroy; 23. often; 24. foolish; 25. 5.7; 26. 0.4; 27. 2.4; 28. 3.0; 29. 8.5; 30. 0.9; 31. 2.15; 32. 0.95; 33. 3.25; 34. 9.89; 35. 7.11; 36. 5.01

Bonus Page 56:
1. s.; 2. F.; 3. i.; 4. J.; 5. q.; 6. L.; 7. c.; 8. H.; 9. x.; 10. X.; 11. b.; 12. S.; 13. h.; 14. K.; 15. j.; 16. P.; 17. r.; 18. W.; 19. t.; 20. D.; 21. o.; 22. B.; 23. g.; 24. U.; 25. y.; 26. N.; 27. d.; 28. I.; 29. w.; 30. R.; 31. m.; 32. T.; 33. u.; 34. C.; 35. e.; 36. M.; 37. n.; 38. G.; 39. k.; 40. V.; 41. p.; 42. E.; 43. v.; 44. A.; 45. a.; 46. Q.; 47. I.; 48. Y.; 49. f.; 50. O

Section 2

Day 1/Page 61:
1. $9\frac{1}{3}$; 2. $3\frac{1}{2}$; 3. $4\frac{3}{4}$; 4. $6\frac{1}{2}$; 5. $4\frac{1}{2}$; 6. 7; 7. $2\frac{1}{3}$; 8. $1\frac{1}{4}$; 9. 4; 10. 8; 11. 16; 12. 36; 13. no; 14. no; 15. yes; Commas are inserted after: 16. Debbie, Don; 17. Bronx, Manhattan, Queens, Brooklyn,; 18. Chinatown, Greenwich Village; 19. – 26. Answers will vary; 27. It has a magnetic field.; 28. the north and south poles; 29. by studying the magnetic particles within rocks

Day 2/Page 63:
1. – 6. Check students' drawings. 1. $\frac{3}{8}$; 2. $\frac{1}{8}$; 3. $\frac{2}{9}$; 4. $\frac{8}{15}$; 5. $\frac{4}{9}$; 6. $\frac{3}{10}$; 7. However; 8. Although; 9. in addition; 10. nevertheless; 11. Moreover; 12. Similarly; 13. C.; 14. from 2600 BCE to 900 CE; 15. Guatemala, Belize, El Salvador, parts of Honduras and southeast Mexico; 16. It had 260 days with a festival every 20th day.; 17. The last sentence suggests that more may be learned about the Maya in the future. It is a good ending because it summarizes the article and hints at what may come next.

Day 3/Page 65:
1. $\frac{3}{10}$; 2. $\frac{4}{9}$; 3. $\frac{8}{35}$; 4. $\frac{1}{18}$; 5. $\frac{5}{36}$; 6. $\frac{1}{7}$; 7. near; 8. behind; 9. under; 10. until; 11. through; 12.–15. Answers will vary; 16. chews; 17. cheap; 18. bear; 19. pale; 20. manor; 21. tiers; 22. 16; 23. Boston Massacre, Boston Tea Party; 24. the Stamp Act, 9 years; 25. King George III; 26. Lexington and Concord

Day 4/Page 67:
1. C; 2. F; 3. A; 4. E; 5. B; 6. D; 7. $\frac{2}{9}$; 8. $\frac{15}{7}$; 9. fraction greater than 1 (sometimes called an improper fraction), $5\frac{3}{5}$, $8\frac{3}{7}$; 10. circled phrases: between the bases, along the trail, until four o'clock, near the window, outside the door, under the house, in the barn; 11. knew, new; 12. hour, our; 13. read; 14. buy, to; 15. their; 16. two; 17. see, sea; 18. tail; 19. B; 20. D; 21. A; 22. E; 23. C

Day 5/Page 69:
1. $\frac{5}{6}$; 2. $1\frac{1}{2}$; 3. $\frac{2}{3}$; 4. 2; 5. $1\frac{1}{5}$; 6. $\frac{1}{3}$; 7. $1\frac{2}{7}$; 8. $\frac{2}{5}$; 9. $\frac{15}{16}$; 10. and; 11. but; 12. and; 13. or; 14. and; 15. but; 16. C; 17. 4, 1, 3, 2; 18. She led American soldiers on a raid.; 19. Answers may include: helped the freed enslaved people, cared for the elderly, worked for women's rights; 20. The author feels that Tubman is an American hero. The author uses words such as strong and brave to describe her.

Answer Key

Day 6/Page 71:
1. 9,373; **2.** 24.683; **3.** 9.096; **4.** 19.14; **5.** 51.841; **6.** $107.02;
7. – 13. Answers will vary; **14.** 1,900,000; **15.** 0.000652; **16.** 54,000,000;
17. 20,100; **18.** 80,000,000; **19.** 7,140; **20.** 0.0000002; **21.** 8.57;
22. 75,000,000,000; **23.** 15,200; **24.** 5,000,000; **25.** 2.3548; Students' writing will vary.

Day 7/Page 73:

Date	Deposit	Withdrawal	Total $
May 15	$500.25	$0	$500.25
May 31	$496.80	$0	$997.05
June 4	$0	$145.00	$852.05
June 15	$435.20	$0	$1,287.25
June 30	$600.00	$0	$1,887.25
July 1	$0	$463.00	$1,424.25
July 15	$110.00	$0	$1,534.25
July 24	$0	$600.00	$934.25

1. iceberg; **2.** seize; **3.** committee; **4.** democratic; **5.** quotation; **6.** sluggish; **7.** oppress; **8.** plaque; **9.** decided; Answer may vary but may include: **10.** mouth; **11.** soup; **12.** painting; **13.** addresses; **14.** gardener; **15.** afternoon; **16.** reasonable; **17.** ad(vertisement); **18.** school; Students' writing will vary.

Day 8/Page 75:
1. 7.055; **2.** 0.7412; **3.** 259.86; **4.** 0.0117; **5.** 0.518; **6.** 0.207; **7.** 0.0007; **8.** 0.275; **9.** S; **10.** P; **11.** H; **12.** M; **13.** S; **14.** H; **15.** P; **16.** M; **17.** Possible answer: the wild geese crying "Spring! It is spring!"; **18.** aloud ringing sound; **19.** Possible answer: The poet feels joyful. She is reflecting the joy she observes in nature. She writes about children dancing and singing, animals singing, and the cold weather leaving. She uses exclamations to show her excitement.

Day 9/Page 77:
1. 0.72; **2.** 0.56; **3.** 13.8; **4.** 40.4; **5.** 53.368; **6.** 365.1232; **7.** 512.05; **8.** 2,514.255; **9.** flour; **10.** lamp; **11.** states; **12.** foot; **13.** go; **14.** vine; **15.** dog; **16.** street (road); **17.** den; **18.** sculpture; **19.** 60 m³; **20.** 160 in.³; **21.** 41.354 m³; **22.** 240 mm³; **23.** 38.4 in.³; **24.** $\frac{3}{32}$ in.³; **25.** 16; **26.** 16; **27.** 1; **28.** 16; **29.** 4; **30.** 112

Day 10/Page 79:
1. 1.8; **2.** 2.6; **3.** 3.7; **4.** 89; **5.** 23.6; **6.** 45.9; **7.** 78.5; **8.** 55.5; **9.** their; **10.** they; **11.** they; **12.** their; **13.** she; **14.** our; **15.** they; **16.** he; **17.** lowest value: 4, highest value: 27, spread: 23, center value: 12; **18.** lowest value: 44, highest value: 52, spread: 8, center value: 48; **19.** lowest value: 10, highest value: 100, spread: 90, center value: 55; earthquake, energy, fault, fracture, focus, above, epicenter, beneath, Seismic waves, Seismologists

Day 11/Page 81:
1. 131.66; **2.** 106,603; **3.** 264,208; **4.** 4,202,534; **5.** 1,328.25; **6.** 9,875.5; **7.** $8\frac{1}{4}$; **8.** $9\frac{3}{20}$; **9.** $5\frac{1}{4}$; **10. – 14.** Answers will vary.; **15.** Answers will vary, but possible answer: It seems like it will be a humorous story. Dr. Dolittle is an odd character who behaves strangely and has animals with funny names.; **16.** The story is told from the third-person point of view. Answers will vary, but possible answer: If Dr. Dolittle told the story, the reader would know more about why he does what he does and what he is thinking.; **17.** Answers will vary.

Day 12/Page 83:
1. – 6. Order of answers may vary: **1.** 78 × 42 = 3,276, 42 × 78 = 3,276, 3,276 ÷ 42 = 78, 3,276 ÷ 78 = 42; **2.** 56 × 39 = 2,184, 2,184 ÷ 39 = 56, 2,184 ÷ 56 = 39; **3.** 27 × 151 = 4,077, 4,077 ÷ 27 = 151, 4,077 ÷ 151 = 27; **4.** 3,762 ÷ 99 = 38, 99 × 38 = 3,762, 38 × 99 = 3,762; **5.** 26,320 ÷ 560 = 47, 47 × 560 = 26,320, 560 × 47 = 26,320; **6.** 48,306 ÷ 582 = 83, 83 × 582 = 48,306, 582 × 83 = 48,306; **7. – 11.** Answers will vary but may include: **7.** She had a pleasant voice.; **8.** The cat has smooth fur.; **9.** The water is shiny and blue.; **10.** Kristen absorbed the information.; **11.** He stood straight.; **12.** Answers will vary. **13.** 9; **14.** 5; **15.** 26; **16.** 89; **17.** 877; **18.** 657; **19.** 200; **20.** 1,395; **21.** 5,529; **22.** 40; **23.** 47,127; **24.** 190,498; Student's writing will vary.

Day 13/Page 85:
1.–8. Possible answers may include: **1.** 4, 6, 8, 10, 12; **2.** 5, 10, 15, 20, 25; **3.** 18, 27, 36, 45, 54; **4.** 24, 36, 48, 60, 72; **5.** 20, 20, 60; **6.** 12, 24, 36; **7.** 10, 20, 30; **8.** 28, 56, 84; **9.** 9; **10.** 18; **11.** 30; **12.** 40; **13.** Carmen walks carefully along the rocky shore.; **14.** Pools of water collect in rocky crevices near the shore.; **15.** Tide pools are home to sea plants and animals.; **16.** Seaweed is the most common tide pool plant.; **17.** They provide food and shelter for a variety of animals.; **18.** Carmen sees spiny sea urchins attached to a rock.; **19.** Their mouths are on their undersides.; **20.** Their sharp teeth cut seaweed into little pieces.; **21. – 26.** Answers will vary.; **27.** 6; **28.** 17; **29.** 1; **30.** 20; **31.** 35; **32.** 34; **33.** 4; **34.** 38; **35.** 74

Day 14/Page 87:
1. $3^3 = 27$; **2.** $2^4 = 16$; **3.** $8^3 = 512$; **4.** $4^6 = 4,096$; **5.** $3^4 = 81$; **6.** $9^3 = 729$; **7.** $10^7 = 10,000,000$; **8.** $5^5 = 3,125$; **9.** CP, planted, raised; **10.** CS, Chinese, Japanese; **11.** N; **12.** CS, Fish, shellfish; **13.** CS, Overfishing, pollution; **14.** CS, Sea farming, ranching; **15.** C; **16.** land and other resources; **17.** They were forced to move if settlers wanted their land.; **18.** lands farther west (Oklahoma); **19.** the long journey west that the Cherokees were forced to make

Day 15/Page 89:
1. herself; **2.** ourselves; **3.** yourself; **4.** herself; **5.** yourselves; **6.** myself; **7.** ✓; **8.** *Wonderama*, which came out last summer, is Ana's favorite movie. **9.** ✓; **10.** The old piano, which was badly in need of tuning, sat in the corner.; **11.** ✓; **12.** My grandmother attended Hawthorne Elementary, which was built in 1928.; **13.** S, trees, soldiers; **14.** S, cars, ants; **15.** M, sound, dogs; **16.** S, clowns, sardines; **17.** M, feet, drums; **18.** students should draw lines around the areas where there are many epicenter symbols; **19.** because one plate is pushed against another

Day 16/Page 91:
1. 128; **2.** 14; **3.** 19; **4.** 26; **5.** 30; **6.** 26; **7.** 126; **8.** 26; **9.** 20; **10.** 64; **11.** 432; **12.** 12; **13.** 104; **14.** 840; **15.** N: 95, 40; **16.** M: 73, N: 68; **17.** M: 70, N: 64, Rule: M - 9 = N; **18.** M: 30, N: 13, Rule: M - 11 = N; **19.** N: 60, 36, Rule: M × 6 = N; **20.** N: 6, 4, Rule: M ÷ 3 = N; **21.** Life, Liberty, and the pursuit of Happiness; **22.** to secure the basic rights of people; **23.** to alter it or abolish it and institute new Government

Day 17/Page 93:
1. 1, 2, 3, 4, 6, 12; 1, 3, 5, 15, Students should circle both 3s.; **2.** 1, 2, 4, 8, 16; 1, 2, 4, 5, 8, 10, 20, 40, Students should circle both 8s.; **3.** 1, 3, 9; 1, 2, 3, 4, 6, 12, Students should circle both 3s.; **4.** 1, 2, 3, 4, 6, 8, 12, 24; 1, 2, 3, 6, 7, 14, 21, 42, Students should circle both 6s.; **5. – 13.** Students should

Answer Key

circle words in blue: **5.** was working; **6.** is walking; **7.** has shopped; **8.** might have called, had known; **9.** is closed; **10.** does enjoy; **11.** is playing; **12.** does finish; **13.** are watching; **14.** B; **15.** World War II; **16.** block proposals brought to the council by voting against them; **17.** 5 years; **18.** Answer may include: provides peacekeepers; helps victims of natural disasters; promotes workers' rights; provides food, medicine, and safe drinking water for those in need.

Day 18/Page 95:
1. $\frac{1}{2}$; **2.** $\frac{4}{1}$; **3.** $\frac{2}{3}$; **4.** $\frac{11}{4}$; **5.** $\frac{8}{3}$; **6.** $\frac{4}{5}$; **7.** The frogs sleep during the day, and they hunt for food at night.; **8.** A parrot's bright colors are easy to see in a tree, but a tree boa's green color makes it difficult to spot.; **9.** A fruit bat has a long nose, and it has large eyes to help it see in the dark.; **10.** I know math well.; **11.** Who told the secret?; **12.** He is just like his father.; **13.** She will sleep very well tonight.; **14.** The two friends are very similar.; **15.** T; **16.** T; **17.** F; **18.** F; **19.** F; **20.** T

Day 19/Page 97:
1. 21 × 13 = (21 × 10) + (21 × 3) = 210 + 63; **2.** 12 × 55 = (12 × 50) + (12 × 5) = 660; **3.** 61 × 15 = (61 × 10) + (61 × 5) = 915; **4.** 45 × 22 = (45 × 20) + (45 × 2) = 990; **5.** 16 × 47 = (16 × 40) + (16 × 7) = 752; **6.** 37 × 102 = (37 × 100) + (37 × 2) = 3,774; **7.** 64 × 13 = (64 × 10) + (64 × 3) = 832; **8.** 48 × 44 = (48 × 40) + (48 × 4) = 2,112; **9.** 33 × 32 = (33 × 30) + (33 × 2) = 1,056; **10.** 216; **11.** 1,050; **12.** 126; **13.** $4,806; **14.** C; **15.** C; **16.** A; **17.** A; **18.** B; **19.** A; Students' writing will vary.

Day 20/Page 99:
1. (3 × a) + 12 = 21 when a = 3; **2.** y × 12 = 108 when y = 9; **3.** 36 ÷ b = 18 when b = 2; **4.** w + 14 = 15 when w = 1; **5.** (z × 6) ÷ 12 = 2 when z = 4; **6.** c^2 × 2 = 50 when c = 5; **7.** (15 − d) ÷ 4 = 2 when d = 7; **8.** 23 + (x ÷ 6) = 25 when x = 12; Answer may vary. Possible answers: therm, heat; biannual; ology, study of; eruption, break; mono, one; ped; **9.** C; **10.** to help predict future weather; **11.** Answers may include: temperature, wind speed, atmospheric pressure, precipitation; **12.** They can predict how climate and weather might change in the future.; **13.** when it might strike and how to stay safe

Bonus Page 103:
1. opinion; **2.** fact; **3.** opinion; **4.** fact; **5.** opinion; **6.** fact; **7.** fact; **8.** opinion

Bonus Page 104:
1. legislative; **2.** legislative; **3.** executive; **4.** judicial; **5.** executive; Pie chart will vary but may include: The executive branch carries out federal laws, recommends new laws, directs national defense and foreign policy, appoints justices, and performs ceremonial duties.; The legislative branch makes laws, passes laws, impeaches officials, and approves treaties.; The judicial branch interprets the Constitution, reviews laws, and decides cases involving states' rights.

Bonus Page 105:
1. Hawaii; **2.** more than 200 inches; **3.** less than 8 inches; **4.** more than 200 inches; **5.** Kamuela; **6.** Flagstaff; **7.** Tucson, Phoenix; **8.** Honokaa, Kailua-Kona

Section 3
Day 1/Page 109:
1. 162 sq. in.; **2.** 330 sq. in.; **3.** 156 sq. cm; **4.** 45 sq. mm; **5.** 26 sq. cm; **6.** 36 sq. mi.; **7.** I; **8.** me; **9.** I; **10.** Her; **11.** his; **12.** mine; **13.** −5, −4, −3, −2, −1; **14.** A; **15.** American Northwest

Day 2/Page 111:
1. OP; **2.** SP; **3.** OP; **4.** SP; **5.** SP; **6.** SP; **7.** SP; **8.** OP; **9.** OP; **10.** SP; **11.** 8; **12.** 8; **13.** 12; **14.** 7; **15.** 15; **16.** 23; **17.** 105; **18.** 48; **19.** 17; **20.** 3; **21.** 62; **22.** 14; **23.** 29; **24.** 82; **25.–26.** Answers will vary; **27.** dramatize, dra-ma-tiz; **28.** 3; **29.** to behave dramatically; **30. – 31.** Answers will vary.; Students' writing will vary.

Day 3/Page 113:
1. 55; **2.** 3.9; **3.** $\frac{3}{4}$ inch; **4.** 17¢; **5.** 1,900; **6.** $4.50; **7.** A, chronology, chronic; **8.** B, astronaut, astronomy; **9.** A, sympathy, empathy; **10.** C, biology, biography; **11.** C; **12.** to buy stamps and mail letters and packages; **13.** on foot, by car, by truck, or by airplane; **14.** a country's national post office; **15.** the size and weight of an item, the distance to its destination, and its target delivery date

Day 4/Page 115:
1. 36x + 15; **2.** 60y − 36; **3.** 40g + 16; **4.** x^2 + 8x; **5.** 75 − 100n; **6.** 32z; **7.** 32x + 52; **8.** 15y + 65; **9.** 8w^2 − 16; **10.** 45c − 30; **11.** 18k − 42; **12.** 12 ÷ 3a; **13.–16.** Answers will vary.; **17.** yes; **18.** yes; **19.** no; **20.** no; **21.** yes; **22.** yes; **23.** yes; **24.** yes; **25.** no; **26.** yes; **27.** no; **28.** no; **29.–30.** Students' sentences will vary.

Day 5/Page 117:
1. $x > 8$;
2. $y < 4$;
3. $d \geq -1$;
4. $a < -2$;
5. $c \leq -8$;
6. $w > 3$;

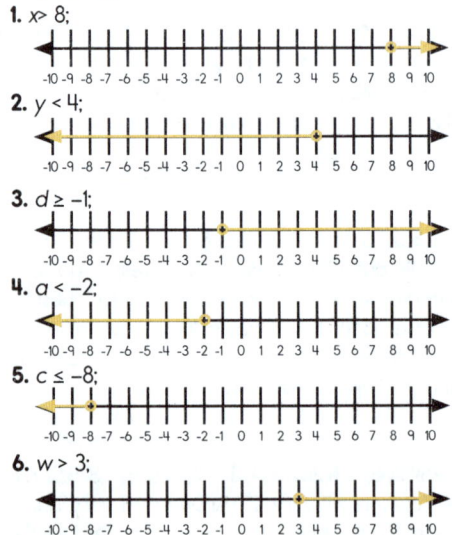

7. D; **8.** H; **9.** A; **10.** F; **11.** G; **12.** C; **13.** E; **14.** B; **15.** horse; **16.** music; **17.** home; **18.** story; **19.** young; **20.** clothing; **21.** 63; **22.** 28; **23.** 56; **24.** 52.3

Day 6/Page 119:
1. 54 bars of soap; **2.** 40 points; **3.** 240 miles; **4.** $9.60, $14.40; **5.** $7.50, $17.50; **6.** $12, $68; **7.** $132, $88; **8.** $49.50, $40.50; **9.** $54, $66;

Answer Key

10. $312.50, $937.50; **11.** C; **12.** for religious freedom or for more land for their families; **13.** horses, oxen, and sheep; **14.** in one-room schoolhouses or at home; **15.** doctor's office, blacksmith's shop, general store

Day 7/Page 121:
1. 1; **2.** 1.5 or $1\frac{1}{2}$; **3.** 24; **4.** 4; **5.** 2; **6.** 21; **7.** 36; **8.** 3; **9.** 9; **10.-15.** Answers will vary, possible answers: **10.** "I really enjoyed the concert," said Marissa. **11.** That construction across the street is bothering me a great deal.; **12.** I appreciate you telling me the recent news.; **13.** We only have a few minutes before the bell, so you have to do it as son as possible.; **14.** A large traffic jam caused traffic to slow down for quite some time.; **15.** "Calm down," said Jaxson, "we have 20 minutes until the bell rings."; **16.** The Table of Contents is arranged by chapters. The Index is arranged alphabetically by subject.; **17.** pages 100-101, 124-130; **18.** in the Table of Contents, Chapter 6, page 260; **19.** 5; **20.** 172

Day 8/Page 123:
1. 250; **2.** 3,000; **3.** 900; **4.** 1,000; **5.** 12,000; **6.** 800; **7.** 5; **8.** 10,000; **9.** 400,000; Answers will vary.; **10.** Timbuktu is a small trading town in central Mali.; **11.** it was a trading post for products from North and West Africa; **12.** Timbuktu's location left it open to attack, and control of the city changed many times.; **13.** 54; **14.** 90; **15.** 158; **16.** 112

Day 9/Page 125:
1. 2; **2.** 48; **3.** 2,000; **4.** 2; **5.** 1; **6.** 6; **7.** 1; **8.** 1; **9.** 0.625 or $\frac{1}{16}$;

1624 Bay Lane
Short Creek, PA 12525
May 10, 2024
Dear Aunt Ann and Uncle Jamal,

  School will soon be out for the summer. I am looking forward to it. The year was good, and I learned a lot.
  Mom and Dad are going to France in July. I don't want to go with them. I'm writing this letter to ask if I can stay with you July 10 through July 22. I would love to help you take care of the horses and do anything else that you would want me to do. I would also help around the house. Please let me know if I can come.

Your loving niece,
Julie Ann

10. 3, 1, 2, 4; **11.** Pulitzer Prize; **12.** families like hers and people who lived in the part of Chicago where she lived; **13.** Answers will vary.

Day 10/Page 127:
1. 1; **2.** 1; **3.** 4,000; **4.** 5,000; **5.** 8,000; **6.** 4; **7.** 9,500; **8.** 2,000,000; **9.** 9; Students' writing will vary **10. – 11.** Answers will vary; **12.** heating and pressure; **13.** melting and crystallization; **14.** sedimentation and compaction; **15.** heating and pressure; **16.** melting and crystallization; **17.** sedimentation and compaction

Day 11/Page 129:
1. 20%; **2.** 50%; **3.** 8%; **4.** 47%; **5.** $\frac{19}{100}$; **6.** $\frac{24}{100}$; **7.** $\frac{87}{100}$; **8.** $\frac{36}{100}$; **9.** $\frac{1}{2}$; **10.** $\frac{9}{10}$; **11.** $\frac{1}{5}$; **12.** $\frac{9}{20}$; **13.** This year, on my nana's birthday (June 14th), we will have a family picnic.; **14.** Jones hit the ball—way into left field—and the crowd went wild.; **15.** The new puppy, a cocker spaniel, got tangled up in its leash.; **16. – 20.** Answer will vary but may include: **16.** pretended; **17.** coworkers; **18.** on time; **19.** stamp collector; **20.** rouse; 3, 1, 2, 4

Day 12/Page 131:
1. $\frac{5}{7}$; **2.** $\frac{20}{13}$; **3.** $\frac{12}{5}$; **4.** $\frac{4}{9}$; **5.** $\frac{23¢}{45¢}$; **6.** $\frac{10}{3}$; **7.** $\frac{1}{4}$; **8.** $\frac{3}{25}$; **9.** $\frac{2}{3}$; **10.** $\frac{3}{2}$; **11.** $\frac{3}{3}$; **12.** $\frac{3}{8}$; **13.** regions; **14.** grip; **15.** primates; **16.** termites; **17.** pokes; **18.** plucks; **19.** charge, ripping; **20.** bounds; **21.** A; **22.** The author's purpose is to explain what geologists do and why it is important. This is evident because the author provides supporting facts and examples.; **23.** movement of plates on Earth's crust, volcanoes, earthquakes, movement of glaciers; **24.** to help plants grow better; **25.** interpret data

Day 13/Page 133:
1. country; **2.** jazz; **3.** 175; **4.** 157.14285; **5.** Answers will vary.; **6.** gigantic; **7.** ornately; **8.** audience; **9.** thirty-year-old; **10.** enormous; **11.** completely; **12.** magnificently; **13.** brilliantly; **14.** enthusiastically; **15.** splendid; **16.** sluggish and lazy (dashes); **17.** flat-bladed ax (phrase); **18.** highly seasoned stew (commas); **19.** kneecap (phrase); **20.** xylophone (parentheses); **21.** effect; **22.** affect; **23.** effect; **24.** affect

Day 14/Page 135:
1. $2.50; **2.** $4.00; **3.** $5.00; **4.** $6.00; **5. – 11.** Answers will vary but may include: **5.** The fight didn't solve anything.; **6.** The team didn't want any trouble.; **7.** Haven't you ever seen Yellowstone National Park?; **8.** There aren't any eggs in the carton.; **9.** He wasn't near any base when he was tagged out.; **10.** There isn't any way to get there from here.; **11.** The explanation didn't make any sense.; **12.** $1\frac{1}{5}$; **13.** 2; **14.** $\frac{2}{9}$; **15.** $\frac{3}{4}$; **16.** B; **17.** D; **18.** C; **19.** A; **20.** E

Day 15/Page 137:
1. Monday; **2.** 10 family members; **3.** 250; **4.** Wednesday; **5.** 55; **6.** Answers will vary.; **7.** Can't anyone solve the puzzle?; **8.** Rick didn't have anything to read.; **9.** There isn't anything you can do about it.; **10.** A; **11.** 2, 4, 1, 3; **12.** New Orleans; **13.** admiral

Day 16/Page 139:
2. (4, 4); **5.** (-9, -4); **8.** trapezoid;

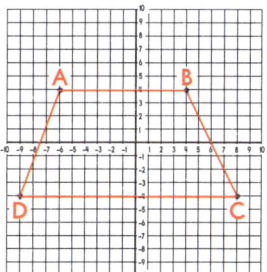

Jokingly named the "Highest Court in the Land," the basketball court and gym on the fifth floor of the United States Supreme Court Building was built in the 1940s. It is located in what used to be a large storage area. No one really knows why the storage area was converted into a gym and basketball court, but it gets used by cafeteria workers, security guards, librarians, law clerks, and even justices who preside over the official Highest Court of the Land. It is rumored that Supreme Court Justices Brett Kavanaugh and Elena Kagan have shot some hoops up here!
9. – 12. Answer will vary but may include: **9.** because, snowstorm,

Answer Key

school was closed; **10.** so, snow, white ground; **11.** so, electricity went out, went out to dinner; **12.** so, unlatched gate, cattle were in the road; **13.** D; **14.** B; **15.** C; **16.** A

Day 17/Page 141:
1. 9; **2.** 0; **3.** -8; **4.** 4; **5.** -2; **6.** <; **7.** >; **8.** >; **9.** <; **10.** >; **11.** >; **12.** Jim, Sean, and Maria liked to visit Grandma and Grandpa.; **13.** Grandma raised chickens, ducks, and geese.; **14.** Daisies, tulips, and roses grew in her garden.; **15. – 23.** Answers will vary.; **24.** Of tennis, baseball, hockey, and karate, I like karate the best.; **25.** I have tried playing the flute, saxophone, drums, violin, and tuba.; **26.** The storm brought hail, sleet, and rain to our town.; **27.** We had to take a train, bus, taxi, and shuttle to get to our destination.

Day 18/Page 143:
1.

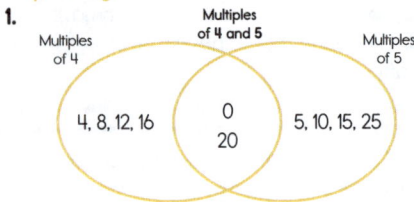

2.

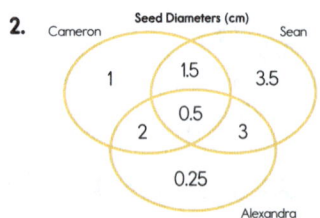

3. her; **4.** his; **5.** her; **6.** my; **7.** her; **8.** their; **9.** Answers will vary.; **10.** Answers will vary. Possible answer: The poet is remembering a time in his life when he made a choice and is grateful that he chose the path he did.; **11.** Answers will vary. Possible answer: The poet looks back on his life and is thankful for the path he chose.

Day 19/Page 145:
1.-4.;

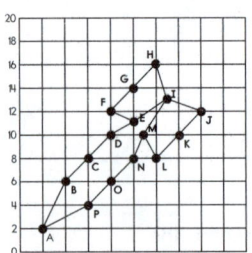

5. Who; **6.** Whom; **7.** Who; **8.** Who; **9.** Who; **10.** Who; **11.** Whom; **12.** who; **13.** trophy, proudly stood; **14.** clouds, spit sleet; **15.** leaves, sing, danced; **16.** Horns, honked angrily; **17.** sun, played hide-and-seek; Students' writing will vary.

Day 20/Page 147:
1.;

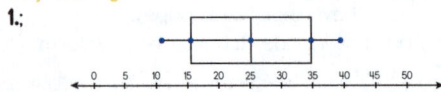

2. 25; **3.** 15; **4.** 35; **5.** lie; **6.** can; **7.** may; **8.** lay; **9.** B; **10.** B; **11.** C; **12.** A; **13.** A; **14.** C; **15.** D; **16.** C; **17.** G; **18.** F; **19.** A; **20.** B; **21.** E

Bonus Page 151:
1. G; **2.** D; **3.** C; **4.** E; **5.** F; **6.** B; **7.** A; **8.** 50, District; **9.** democracy, president; **10.** legislature, governor

Bonus Page 152:
1. no; **2.** no; **3.** yes; **4.** yes; **5.** no; **6.** no; **7.** no; **8.** yes

Bonus Page 153:
1. false; **2.** true; **3.** false; **4.** true; **5.** false; **6.** true; **7.** false; **8.** true; **9.** true; **10.** false

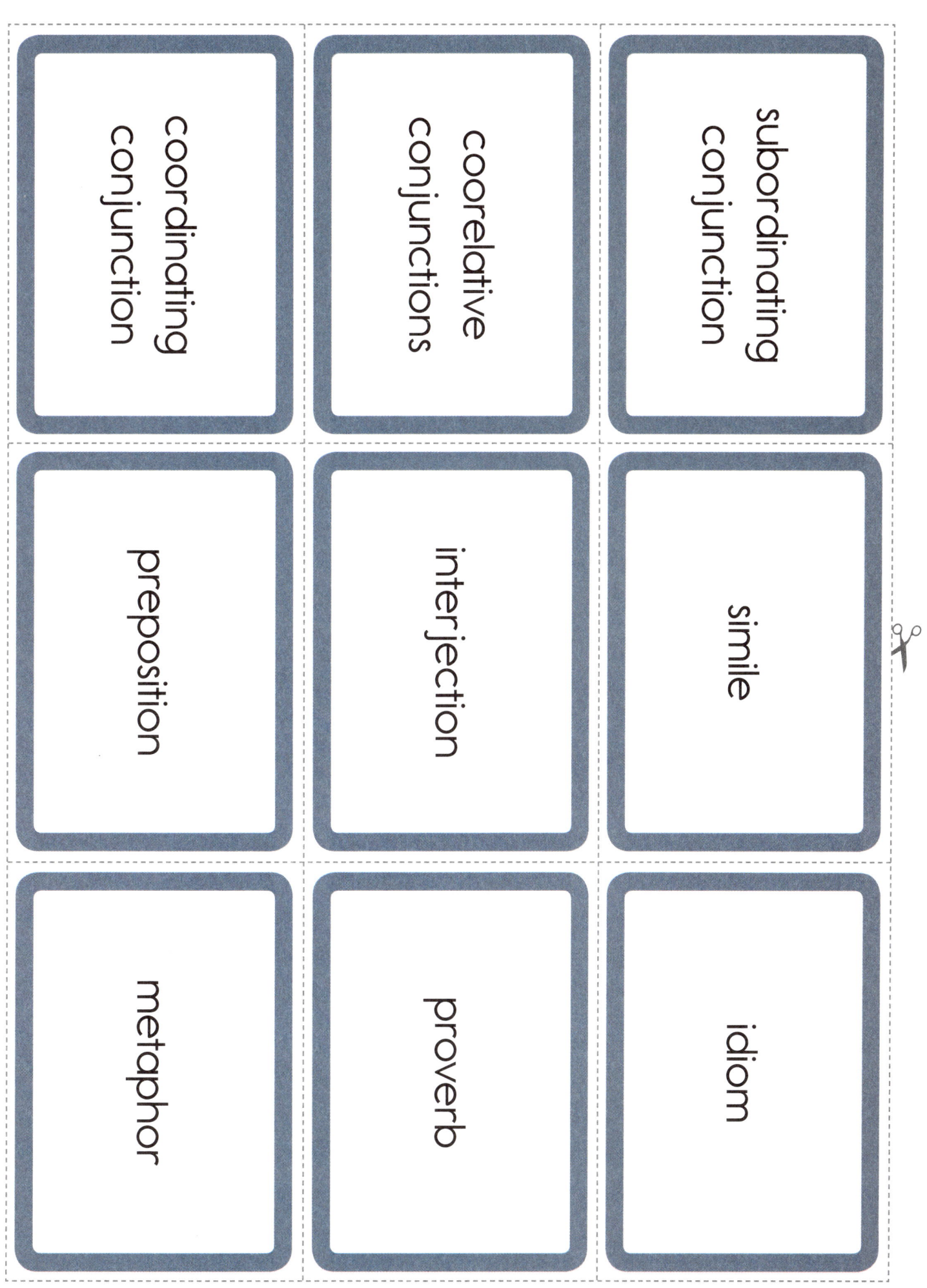

combines two independent clauses with a conjunction and a comma	pairs of words that connect other parts of a sentence	a word or phrase that links a dependent clause to an independent clause
a word that tells us where or when something is in relation to something else	a word or phrase that expresses surprise or strong emotion	compares two things using *like* or *as*
compares two things without using *like* or *as*	a short saying that expresses a general truth	a short saying that is not meant to be taken literally

superlative adjective	comparative adjective	hyperbole
indefinite pronoun	relative pronoun	possessive pronoun
affect vs. *effect*	semi-colon ;	colon :

compares three or more things, uses *most* or *-est*	compares two things, uses *more* or *-er*	an exaggeration that is obviously not true
a nonspecific pronoun	connects a noun with an adjective clause	shows ownership
affect is a verb, *effect* is a noun	used to separate parts of a sentence; stronger than a comma	used to introduce a list of items, to separate clauses, or for emphasis

opinion writing	informative writing	*than* vs. *then*
historical fiction	fable	narrative writing
obtuse angle	acute angle	poetry

writing that expresses an opinion	writing that is meant to inform or teach	*than* compares two things, *then* relates to time or order of events
writing that is fictional but based on real events that happened in history	writing that is fictional, teaches a moral or lesson, and usually includes animals as characters	writing that tells a story
measures more than 90° but less than 180°	measures between 0° and 90°	writing that is typically written in verses and uses figurative language

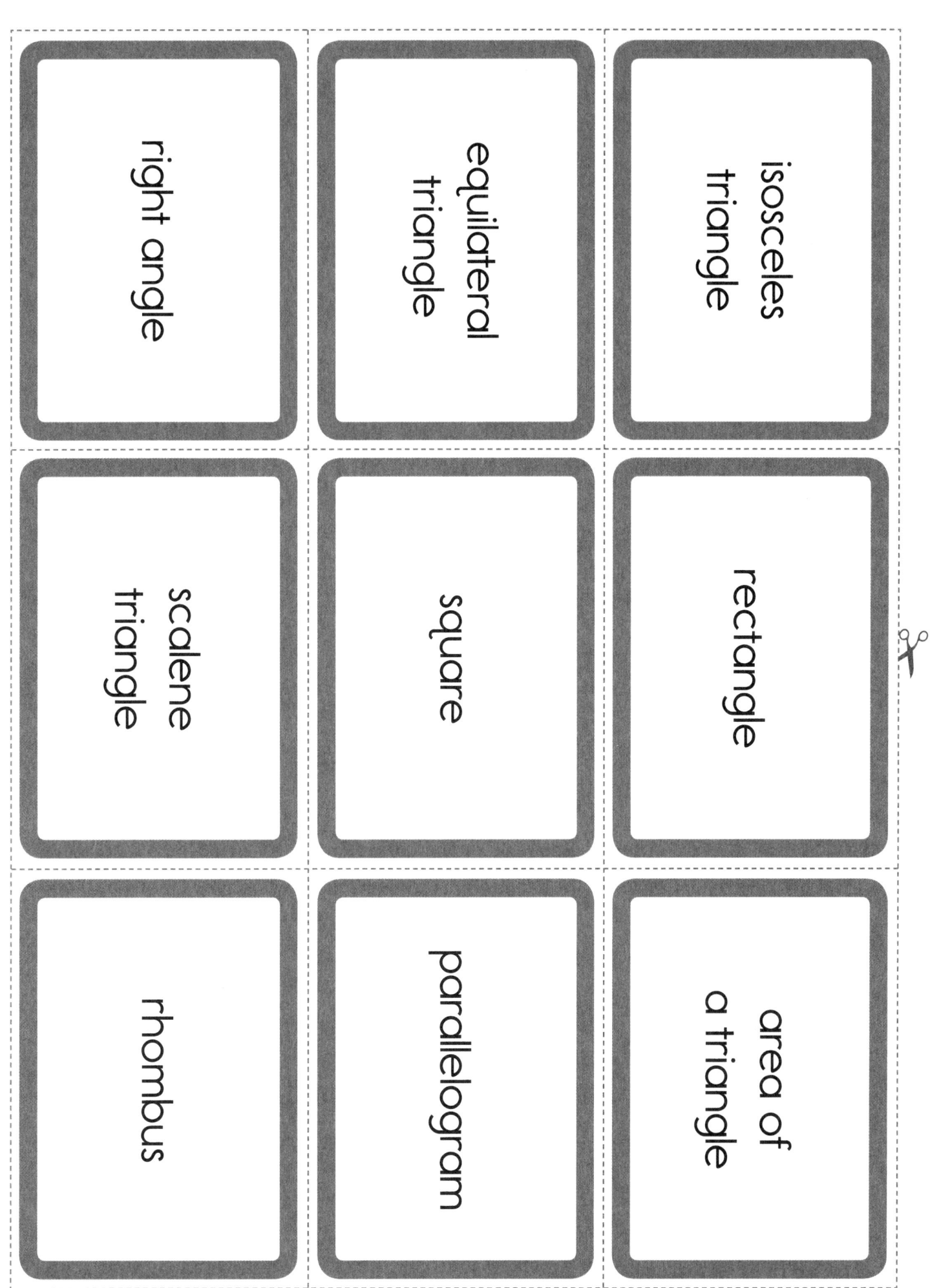

measures 90°	all 3 sides have the same length	2 congruent side lengths and base angles
no equal side lengths	parallelogram with 4 congruent sides, 4 interior right angles	2 pairs of congruent opposite sides, 4 interior right angles
4 congruent sides, opposite angles are equal	congruent opposite sides, opposite angles are equal	$A = \frac{1}{2} b \times h$

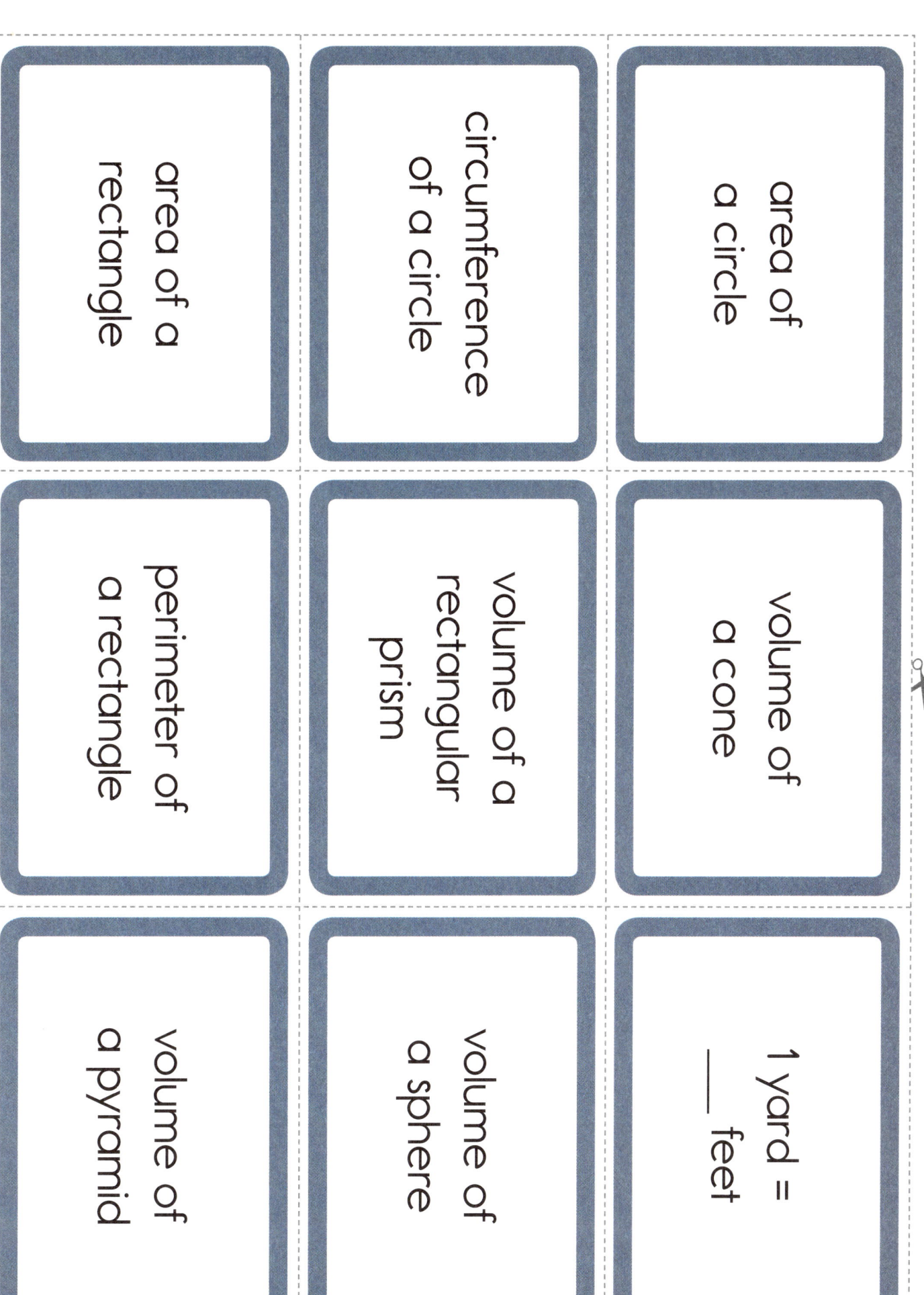

$A = l \times w$	$C = \pi d$	$A = \pi r^2$
$P = 2l + 2w$	$V = l \times w \times h$	$V = \frac{1}{3}\pi r^2 h$
$V = \frac{1}{3}Bh$ (where B = area of base)	$V = \frac{4}{3}\pi r^3$	$\frac{3}{4}$ feet

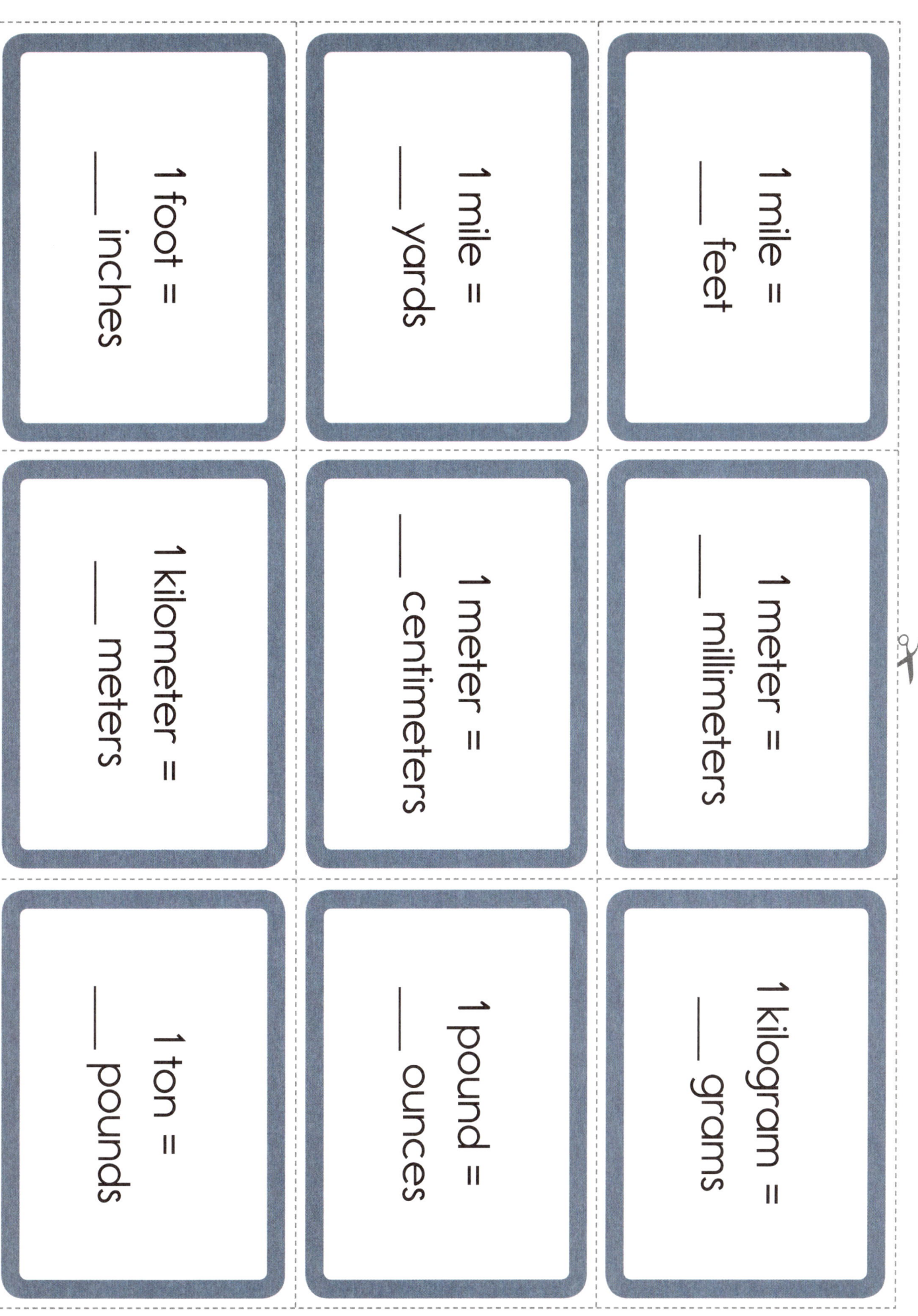

1 gallon = ___ quarts

1 gallon = ___ pints

1 gallon = ___ cups

distributive property

associative property

mean

median

mode

range

4 quarts	8 pints	16 cups
a (b × c) = ab + ac, a (b - c) = ab - ac	(x + y) + z = x + (y + z)	the average of a data set: add up all numbers, divide by how many numbers
the middle value when the data set is ordered from least to greatest	the number that occurs most often in a data set	the difference between the highest and lowest numbers in a data set

Math Key Words

Addition +	Subtraction −
add	subtract
sum	difference
plus	left
total	minus
combine	left over
increase	take away
more	decrease
all together	fewer

Multiplication ×	Division ÷
product	divide
times	share
factor	split
groups	quotient
double	average
each	each
rows	equal groups
area	separate

Multiplication Table

×	1	2	3	4	5	6	7	8	9	10	11	12
1	1	2	3	4	5	6	7	8	9	10	11	12
2	2	4	6	8	10	12	14	16	18	20	22	24
3	3	6	9	12	15	18	21	24	27	30	33	36
4	4	8	12	16	20	24	28	32	36	40	44	48
5	5	10	15	20	25	30	35	40	45	50	55	60
6	6	12	18	24	30	36	42	48	54	60	66	72
7	7	14	21	28	35	42	49	56	63	70	77	84
8	8	16	24	32	40	48	56	64	72	80	88	96
9	9	18	27	36	45	54	63	72	81	90	99	108
10	10	20	30	40	50	60	70	80	90	100	110	120
11	11	22	33	44	55	66	77	88	99	110	121	132
12	12	24	36	48	60	72	84	96	108	120	132	144

Fraction Operations

Addition	Subtraction
same denominators $\frac{a}{b} + \frac{c}{b} = \frac{a+c}{b}$	same denominators $\frac{a}{b} - \frac{c}{b} = \frac{a-c}{b}$
different denominators $\frac{a}{b} + \frac{c}{d} = \frac{ad+bc}{bd}$	different denominators $\frac{a}{b} - \frac{c}{d} = \frac{ad-bc}{bd}$

Multiplication	Division
$\frac{a}{b} \times \frac{c}{d} = \frac{ac}{bd}$	$\frac{a}{b} \div \frac{c}{d} = \frac{a}{b} \times \frac{d}{c} = \frac{ad}{bc}$

Place Value

millions , hundred thousands | ten thousands | thousands , hundreds | tens | ones . tenths | hundredths | thousandths

"million"   "thousand"   "and"

Each place has a value that is **10 times as great** as the place value to the right.

÷ 10 →
← × 10

$2.41 \div 10^2$
0.02.41
0.0241

2.41×10^4
2.4100.
24,100

Exponential Form	Standard Form
10^1	10
10^2	100
10^3	1,000
10^4	10,000
10^5	100,000
10^6	1,000,000

Tricky Words

- **accept** — to receive
- **except** — not including
- **affect** — verb, to create change
- **effect** — noun, the change itself
- **buy** — to purchase
- **by** — close to
- **bye** — goodbye
- **its** — owned by it
- **it's** — it is
- **lay** — to put or place
- **lie** — resting position
- **then** — at that time
- **than** — a comparison
- **there** — a place
- **their** — owned by them
- **they're** — they are
- **to**
- **too** — also, very
- **two** — 2
- **your** — owned by you
- **you're** — you are

More Tricky Words

- **break** — to split
- **brake** — to stop
- **passed** — moved by
- **past** — time that has gone by
- **weather** — outdoor conditions
- **whether** — introduces a choice
- **dessert** — a food
- **desert** — a place
- **principal** — a head of a school
- **principle** — a standard or rule
- **whose** — shows belonging
- **who's** — who is
- **lose** — to misplace
- **loose** — not tight
- **wear** — to put on clothing
- **where** — in what location
- **were** — past tense of are
- **we're** — we are

Things Good Readers Do

Preview	• Look at the cover. • Read the title and some of the text.
Question	• Ask who, what, when, where, why, and how. • Decide if the text makes sense.
Predict	• Wonder about what will happen. • Make predictions and read to see if they are correct.
Infer	• Think about what the details tell you. • Use the details to understand what the author means.
Connect	• Relate the text to your thoughts and feelings. • Compare the text to other texts and the world around you.
Summarize	• Organize the main details. • Draw conclusions.
Evaluate	• Think about what you learned. • Decide if what you read was important. • Decide if you enjoyed the text.

The Writing Process

- **Prewriting:** thinking about a topic, brainstorming, and planning
- **Drafting:** quickly putting thoughts on paper
- **Revising:** reworking the organization and details
- **Editing:** reviewing and correcting spelling, grammar, capitalization, and punctuation
- **Evaluating:** reflecting and assessing what has been written
- **Publishing:** sharing final writing with others